Anonymous

Springs in the Desert for Christ's Flock

Anonymous

Springs in the Desert for Christ's Flock

ISBN/EAN: 9783337369262

Printed in Europe, USA, Canada, Australia, Japan

Cover: Foto ©Andreas Hilbeck / pixelio.de

More available books at **www.hansebooks.com**

SPRINGS IN THE DESERT

FOR

CHRIST'S FLOCK.

BY

M. J. H. P.

LONDON:

JOHN F. SHAW AND CO.,

48 PATERNOSTER ROW.

1864.

INTRODUCTION.

To the "Church in the Wilderness," the pilgrim band now experiencing the vicissitudes of desert-life,—to the tried, the tempted, the suffering believer, this little work is affectionately addressed by a "companion in tribulation," who prays that the humble effort to comfort His sorrowing ones may be owned and blessed by the great Head of the Church, "to whom be glory forever. Amen."

CONTENTS.

CHAPTER I.

Abiding in Jesus.

"Abide in me, and I in you. As the branch cannot bear fruit of itself, except it abide in the vine ; no more can ye, except ye abide in me. I am the vine, ye are the branches : he that abideth in me, and I in him, the same bringeth forth much fruit : for without me ye can do nothing."—JOHN xv. 4, 5.

" He that saith he abideth in him ought himself also so to walk even as he walked."—1 JOHN ii. 6.

" For we are made partakers of Christ, if we hold the beginning of our confidence steadfast unto the end."—HEB. iii. 14.

" If ye continue in the faith grounded and settled, and be not moved away from the hope of the gospel, which ye have heard."—COL. i. 23.

" And we desire that every one of you do shew the same diligence to the full assurance of hope unto the end."—HEB. vi. 11.

" Cast not away therefore your confidence, which hath great recompense of reward."—HEB. x. 35.

A

" O Lamb of God ! still keep me
    Near to Thy wounded side ;
'Tis only there in safety
    And peace I can abide.
What foes and snares surround me !
    What lusts and fears within !
The grace that sought and found me
    Alone can keep me clean.

" 'Tis only in Thee hiding,
    I feel my life secure ;
Only in Thee abiding,
    The conflict can endure.
Thine arm the victory gaineth
    O'er every hateful foe ;
Thy love my heart sustaineth
    In all its care and woe.

" Soon shall my eyes behold Thee
    With rapture face to face ;
One half hath not been told me
    Of all Thy power and grace.
Thy beauty, Lord, and glory,
    The wonders of Thy love,
Shall be the endless story
    Of all Thy saints above."

" NOW ye are clean through the word which I have spoken unto you," (John xv. 3.)

Such were some of the parting words of Jesus to His disciples. The truth had "made them free;" through faith they had been united to the "living vine;" so closely and indissolubly joined to Christ, as to be members of His body. The word spoken unto them by their Lord had become, through the power of the Holy Ghost, a living seed, "springing up into everlasting life." Their salvation was as secure as the covenant between the Father and the Son, confirmed by the blood of Jesus, could make it. They were as safe as if already in heaven. Wonderful, yet true! True of the disciples, and no less true of the weakest believer in Jesus, who, having discovered his own vileness, has touched the hem of Christ's garment, it may be with fear and trembling, yet with the faith which is *never* unacknowledged, *never* sent empty away. We are, at the beginning of our Christian course, *quickened* by faith, and the life which we then receive, and which is eternal as God himself, is, throughout the whole of our pilgrimage here, to be *maintained* and *renewed* by faith, until it is perfected in heaven. The work of *sanctification* in the heart of a believer depends as entirely upon his *abiding* in Jesus by faith, as did the work of *justification* upon his simply looking to Jesus in faith; and in *both* must the eternal Spirit exercise His quickening power, or the truths of the gospel will be but "a savour of death unto death."

"Being justified by faith, we have peace with God." We are at once and for ever freed from condemnation, and made "joint-heirs with Christ,"—our sins blotted out for ever, and "cast into the depths of the sea."

By Christ "we have also *access* by faith into this grace wherein we stand."

We need, moment by moment, a strength not in ourselves, to *maintain* the life already begun in our souls. This strength lies in Jesus, and we have access to it by faith.

Thus are we *made alive* and *kept alive*
by faith. It was not until the Holy
Spirit taught us the necessity of "ceasing from our own works," and resting
wholly upon the finished work of Jesus,
that we obtained "peace with God;"
and just in proportion as the believer
realises the truth, that the life begun in
his soul must be maintained by continual *abiding* in Jesus, will he *enjoy* the
"peace which passeth all understanding." Here, amid all the din and turmoil of this evil world, there is rest and
peace for the believer. Hidden in the
heart of Jesus, joined to Him by the
closest union, he already by faith "beholds the land that is very far off," and
is blessed with a foretaste of his eternal
rest. His life is the life of Christ
himself, beating in every pulse of his

spiritual being. "Your life is hid with Christ in God." What blessed, what perfect security!

"We which have believed *do* enter into rest." We are still dwelling in the midst of a "world lying in wickedness." We still carry within us a body of sin, and to a certain extent our great adversary still has the power of harassing and tempting us; yet, in spite of all, it is the believer's happy privilege already to "rejoice with joy unspeakable, and full of glory,"—already by faith to "come unto Mount Sion, the city of the living God, the heavenly Jerusalem."

"But why," it may be asked, "do many sincere souls experience so little of this joy?"

We answer in the Lord's own words: "Because of their unbelief."

They do not "hold the *beginning* of their confidence steadfast unto the end." They suffer themselves to be "moved away from the hope of the gospel," and although, having come to Jesus in faith, they *have received* eternal life, and can *never* perish, they lose much of the joy and peace which are their *present* portion, because they do not habitually and unceasingly *live* upon Jesus by faith; just as in the beginning of their Christian course, they were saved by faith.

There is also much self-righteousness remaining in the hearts even of the Lord's own people, and, hardly conscious of it themselves, many believers have an idea, that although in the work of *justification* their salvation consists in "ceasing from their own works," and resting solely upon the perfect work of Jesus, yet that their *sanctification* depends in some measure upon their own efforts, aided by the Holy Spirit. Now that the Holy Spirit *does* carry on the work of sanctification within the believer's heart, we do not for one moment deny; but the grace, wisdom, and strength, which we continually need, are all laid up in *Jesus,* "who of God is made unto us wisdom, and righteousness, and *sanctification,* and redemption." The believer has no more power in *himself* to bring forth fruit unto God, than he had, as a poor, ruined sinner, power to save himself from condemnation. From first to last Christ Jesus must be his all in all, his Alpha and Omega, "the Author and Finisher of his faith," and, thus *abiding* in Jesus, his course through this world will be like the walk of Enoch—a

course of holy, unhindered communion
with his God and *Saviour.*

" Thou Shepherd of Israel, and mine,
    The joy and desire of my heart,
For closer communion I pine,
    I long to reside where Thou art.
The pasture I languish to find,
    Where all who their Shepherd obey
Are fed, on Thy bosom reclined—
    Secure from the heat of the day.

" Ah ! shew me that happiest place,
    The place of Thy people's abode,
Where saints in an ecstasy gaze,
    And hang on a crucified God.
Thy love to a sinner declare,
    Thy passion and death on the tree ;
My spirit to Calvary bear,
    To suffer and triumph with Thee.

" 'Tis there, with the lambs of Thy flock,
    There only I covet to rest—
To lie at the foot of the rock,
    Or rise to be hid in Thy breast.
'Tis there I would always abide,
    And ne'er for a moment depart,
Conceal'd in the cleft of Thy side,
    Eternally hid in Thy heart."

CHAPTER II.

The Fountain Opened.

"In that day there shall be a fountain opened to the house of David and to the inhabitants of Jerusalem for sin and for uncleanness."—ZECH. xiii. 1.

"Speak unto the children of Israel, that they bring thee a red heifer without spot, wherein is no blemish, and upon which never came yoke: and ye shall give her unto Eleazar the priest, that he may bring her forth without the camp, and one shall slay her before his face: and Eleazar the priest shall take of her blood with his finger, and sprinkle of her blood directly before the tabernacle of the congregation seven times: and one shall burn the heifer in his sight; her skin, and her flesh, and her blood, with her dung, shall he burn: and the priest shall take cedar wood, and hyssop, and scarlet, and cast it into the midst of the burning of the heifer. . . . And a man that is clean shall gather up the ashes of the heifer, and lay them up without the camp in a clean place, and it shall be kept for the congregation of the children of Israel for a water of separation: it is a purification for sin. . . . He that toucheth the dead body of any man shall be unclean seven days. . . . And whosoever toucheth one that is slain with a sword in the open fields, or a dead body, or a bone of a man, or a grave, shall be unclean seven days. And for an unclean person they shall take of the ashes of the burnt heifer of purification for sin, and running water shall be put thereto in a vessel: and a clean person shall take hyssop, and dip it in the water, and sprinkle it upon the tent, and upon all the vessels, and upon the persons that were there, and upon him that touched a bone, or one slain, or one dead, or a grave."—NUM. xix. 2-6, 9, 11, 16-18.

"If the blood of bulls and of goats, and the ashes of an heifer sprinkling the unclean, sanctifieth to the purifying of the flesh: how much more shall the blood of Christ, who through the eternal Spirit offered himself without spot to God, purge your conscience from dead works to serve the living God."—HEB. ix. 13, 14.

"The blood of Jesus Christ his Son cleanseth us from all sin."—1 JOHN i. 7.

" The fountain of Christ, Lord, help us to sing,
The blood of our Priest, our crucified King,
Which perfectly cleanses from sin and from guilt,
And richly dispenses salvation and health.

" This fountain so dear, He 'll freely impart,
Unlock'd by the spear, it gush'd from His heart,
With blood and with water—the *first* to *atone*,
To *cleanse* us the *latter*,—the fountain's but one.

" This fountain from guilt not only makes pure,
But gives, soon as felt, infallible cure ;
Whatever diseases or dangers befall,
The fountain of Jesus doth rid us of all.

" This fountain, though rich, from charge is quite free,
The poorer the wretch the welcomer he ;
Here's strength for the weakly that hither are led,
Here's health for the sickly, here 's life for the dead.

" This fountain in vain has never been tried ;
It takes out all stain whenever applied ;
The water flows sweetly with virtue divine,
To cleanse souls completely, though leprous as mine."

HART.

OW continually does the believer feel his need of daily and hourly cleansing! Passing through a world full of pollution, and carrying within him a heart prone to wander from Jesus, he is ever contracting defilement, which, unless washed away in the "fountain opened for sin and for uncleanness," hinders his joy, and disturbs his peace. It is the *privilege* of the saint of God to *rejoice*, to dwell in the sunshine of his Father's reconciled countenance, to breathe a heavenly atmosphere, to hold unbroken fellowship with his Saviour. But, alas! how often does sin cast its dark shadow on the soul, and mar its serenity! How often does its hateful presence in some corner of the heart bring guilt upon the conscience, and a burden on the spirit! Wherever this is the case, and sin is suffered to remain in the heart unacknowledged, instead of being at once carried in humble confession to Jesus, there can be no happy communion with the Saviour, no enjoyment in prayer, no delight in the word ; but the soul will be burdened, joyless, and cast down, until there has been a fresh application by faith to the atoning blood, the same precious blood which gave us peace when, as ruined sinners, we came at *first* to its cleansing stream. Under the Levitical dispensation, a remarkable provision was made for the children of Israel, in "the water of separation." A red heifer without spot or blemish was to be slain, and afterwards burnt with fire. The ashes were then to be gathered up, and "*kept* for the congregation of the children of Israel for a water of separation, a purification for sin." *Constant* recourse was had to the "water of separation," for the slightest *contact* with defilement rendered it necessary for an Israelite to repair to the cleansing water; otherwise he was cut off from his peculiar rights and privileges as one of the chosen people of God. This Levitical law beautifully illustrates the blessed efficacy of Christ's blood, not only as a ransom for sin, but as a fountain to which His chosen ones may continually resort, when the slightest stain upon the conscience warns them that they have contracted pollution by touching the unclean thing. Death in any form was pollution to the Israelite. The mere touching of a bone, or a grave, made him unclean. To the believer, who has been *quickened* by the Spirit, who is already one of the "*living* stones" in Christ's temple, who *has* "passed from death unto life," any union or conformity of spirit to a world "dead in trespasses and sins," is loathsome and defiling as the presence of death. Life and death *cannot* amalgamate. "The friendship of this world is enmity with God," and where worldliness in any form has been allowed admittance into the heart of a true child of God, the conscience *must* remain burdened and uneasy, until the stain of sin has been removed. Whenever, too, through the unwatchfulness of a careless walk, the believer has been overtaken by sin, and the old man within him has been suffered to gain the ascendancy, instead of being habitually crucified and counted as a dead thing, there will be a painful sense of guilt, a consciousness of some cloud between the soul and Jesus, an absence of spiritual joy; and just as the Israelite who had contracted defilement was "cut off from among the congregation," until the "water of separation" had been sprinkled upon him, so will the careless, unwatchful believer lose the peace which is his portion and privilege, until his "heart has been sprinkled from an evil conscience," and every trace of sin has been removed from his soul. In the use of

B

the "water of separation," there is one point to be especially noticed. Running or *living* water was always to be added to the ashes of the heifer, and the person or thing to be cleansed, sprinkled from a bunch of hyssop dipped into it. In the Word of God, water is frequently used as an emblem of the Holy Spirit: "He that believeth on me, as the Scripture hath said, out of his belly shall flow rivers of *living* water. But this spake he of the Spirit, which they that believe on him should receive," (John vii. 38, 39.) How strikingly does the *running* water, which was a necessary part of the purification, set forth our need of the blessed Spirit, without whom we cannot come to Christ; without whose aid the cleansing stream will flow from us in vain. It was the Spirit who first convinced us of sin, and led us to Jesus. It is He who "takes of the things of Christ and shews them unto us." Without His teaching the Bible is but a sealed book to us, and its precious truths only a dead letter. Without His power we cannot abide in Jesus, or bring forth fruit unto God, or realise by faith "the things which God hath prepared for them that love Him." His indwelling presence must guide and support us throughout the whole of our wilderness journey, or we can never gain our heavenly inheritance.

Oh that we may never *grieve* this holy loving Spirit, by a careless unholy walk, by indulgence in sin, by anything unbecoming in the purchased people of Christ! What an inestimable blessing is it to possess a tender conscience, to detect the smallest cloud between our souls

and Jesus, and to be restless and uneasy
until it is removed! To feel conscious
when our communion with the Beloved
has been interrupted, and to lose no time
in repairing to the " blood of sprinkling,"
that we may be once more restored to
His embrace, and rest in the assurance
of His precious unchangeable love! O
believer! dwell not so much upon *your*
love to Jesus, as upon *His* love to *you.*
" The same yesterday, to-day, and for
ever," *His* love never fluctuates. In
spite of our wanderings, our follies, our
sins, it still remains the same. " Having
loved his own, he loved them unto the
end." The devil would fain make us believe, when by his craft and malice he has
drawn us into sin, that the Lord loves us
less ; but oh no! His heart still yearns
over us with a love which no folly of ours

can impair or extinguish ; and although He may chasten and smite us, the sharpest stroke and the bitterest cup is administered by the same tender, changeless love, which constrained Him to give His own life for our ransom.

"O my Saviour crucified !
Near Thy cross would I abide,
There to look with steadfast eye
On Thy dying agony.

"Jesus, bruised and put to shame,
Tells me all Jehovah's name ;
God is love, I surely know,
By the Saviour's depths of woe.

"In His spotless soul's distress,
I perceive my guiltiness ;
Oh, how vile my lost estate
Since my ransom was so great !

"Dwelling thus on Calvary,
Contrite shall my spirit be ;
Rest and holiness shall find,
Fashion'd like my Saviour's mind."

CHAPMAN.

CHAPTER III.

𝕱𝖆𝖎𝖙𝖍.

"Therefore being justified by faith, we have peace with God through our Lord Jesus Christ : by whom also we have access by faith into this grace wherein we stand, and rejoice in hope of the glory of God."—ROM. v. 1, 2.

" Now faith is the substance of things hoped for, the evidence of things not seen."—HEB. xi. 1.

"If ye have faith, and doubt not, ye shall not only do this which is done to the fig-tree, but also if ye shall say unto this mountain, Be thou removed, and be thou cast into the sea : it shall be done.   And all things, whatsoever ye shall ask in prayer *believing*, ye shall receive."—MATT. xxi. 21, 22.

"Watch ye, stand fast in the faith, quit you like men, be strong."—1 COR. xvi. 13.

" According to your faith be it unto you."—MATT. ix. 29.

" Knowing this, that the trying of your faith worketh patience."—JAMES i. 3.

"That the trial of your faith, being much more precious than of gold that perisheth, though it be tried with fire, might be found unto praise and honour and glory at the appearing of Jesus Christ : whom having not seen, ye love ; in whom, though now ye see him not, yet believing, ye rejoice with joy unspeakable and full of glory : receiving the end of your faith, even the salvation of your souls."—1 PET. i. 7-9.

"Let us lay aside every weight, and the sin which doth so easily beset us, and let us run with patience the race that is set before us, looking unto Jesus the author and finisher of our faith."—HEB. xii. 1, 2.

" Lord, increase our faith."—LUKE xvii. 5.

" Faith adds new joy to earthly bliss,
　　And saves us from its snares,
Fresh aid in every duty brings,
　　And softens all our cares.

" Faith draws aside the veil of heaven,
　　Where unknown glories reign ;
And bids us seek our portion there,
　　Nor bids us seek in vain.

" Faith holds to view the promise, seal'd
　　With the Redeemer's blood,
And helps our feeble hope to rest
　　Upon a faithful God.

" There, there unshaken may we rest,
　　Till this vile body dies ;
And then, on Faith's triumphant wings,
　　To endless glory rise !"

IT is by *faith* that the awakened sinner first draws near to Jesus. His sins, "as a heavy burden," overwhelm his soul, he groans beneath them, longs for deliverance, but can find no comfort, till faith leads him to the cross, and points to his bleeding Saviour. There he beholds his iniquities laid upon the Lamb of God, while, at the same moment, his own "shoulder is delivered from the burden," and he no longer bows beneath its pressure, for his "sins are cast into the depths of the sea," to be remembered no more.

Then hope springs up in his soul, and peace imparts a holy calmness to his whole inner being, while the same heart which was once the habitation of the evil one, becomes a "temple of the Holy Ghost."

Thus saved from eternal death, and for ever delivered from his burden, the new-born soul "goes on his way rejoicing," no longer wearing his own "filthy rags," but clothed in the spotless robe of his Saviour's righteousness, and, turning his back upon the world, begins his march to Zion, faith supporting his inexperienced steps in the way of holiness.

As he proceeds on his journey, each day's experience teaches him the indispensable need of *faith*. He discovers that the new life upon which he has just entered, can only be sustained by *faith*,

that in *himself* he possesses no resources
whatever, but that all his supplies must
be obtained from the fulness of Christ.
He finds that if, for a single moment,
he forgets his own weakness, and looks
away from Jesus, failure and sin are the
results, but that victory, joy, and peace
are the unfailing consequences of a steadfast reliance on his Saviour. He feels
that he has no power of his *own* to
"crucify the lusts of the flesh," and yet
that he cannot retain his "joy and peace
in believing," unless they are habitually
and rigidly mortified and held in subjection. This discovery again obliges him
to obtain by faith the grace and strength
needed for this unceasing conflict. Thus,
from his inmost soul, he realises the truth
of the Apostle's words, "I am crucified
with Christ : nevertheless I live ; yet not

I, but Christ liveth in me : and the life which I now live in the flesh I live by the faith of the Son of God, who loved me, and gave himself for me."

As this life has been begun by faith, so must it be *continued* by faith. "Through faith we overcome the wicked one ;" by faith we triumph over tribulation ; by faith we are blessed even in this life with a foretaste of eternal joys ; by faith we grow in the knowledge and love of Jesus ; and in faith we wait for the full accomplishment of those "great and precious promises," which sustain the child of God through the present scene of trial.

"I find," writes a believer, "that while faith is steady, nothing can disquiet me, and when faith totters nothing can establish me." But, alas ! of how many Christians may it be asked, "Why art thou, being a king's son, *lean* from day to day ?"

God never stints His children. He delights to feed them with heavenly food —with royal dainties. It is their privilege " to sit every day at the king's table." His invitation is, " Eat, O friends ; drink, yea, drink abundantly, O beloved." But, He will be inquired of ; He will not bestow His blessings upon the slothful and careless. His promise is accompanied by a condition : " *Ask*, and it shall be given you ; *seek*, and ye shall find ; *knock*, and it shall be opened to you." But how do we ask ? Too often carelessly, coldly, without faith, without energy. No wonder, then, that we " receive not, because we ask amiss." It is to the prayer of *faith alone*, that God sends an answer. " Let us, therefore, come boldly unto the

throne of grace." Without faith we cannot come boldly. We shall come doubt-
ingly and fearfully, instead of *expecting*
and *looking out* for an answer.

" If any of you lack wisdom, let him
ask of God, that giveth to all men liber-
ally, and upbraideth not; and it shall be
given him. But let him *ask in faith,
nothing wavering.* For he that wavereth
is like a wave of the sea driven with the
wind and tossed. For let not that man
think that he shall receive anything of
the Lord."

Can anything be more unstable than
a wave of the sea? Always in motion,
never at rest, it is in a state of perpetual
disquiet, yet is it a just picture of the
Christian whose faith is feeble and un-
settled. Where there is a lack of faith
there must be a lack of every other

Christian grace. Faith is a master-key, by which alone we have access to the treasury of Christ's fulness. "Faith is the substance of things hoped for,"—that is, the *ground* or *confidence*,—so that by faith, we already, in a measure, enjoy the blessings for which we wait, feeling so unquestionably *assured* that they shall be ours, that it is like present possession. "Faith is the evidence of things not seen." It is the earnest of our heavenly inheritance, the germ of a flower which is to expand in eternity.

O believer! *pray* for the *increase* of this precious fruit of the Spirit. Rest not satisfied with a *small* measure, with just sufficient faith to secure salvation, but seek to be "*strong* in faith, giving glory to God."

The Lord is never more glorified

in His people, than when their faith (which is His own gift) triumphs over all obstacles, all difficulties, all temptations.

> "Faith, mighty faith, the *promise* sees,
> And looks to that alone ;
> Laughs at impossibilities,
> And says, "It *shall* be done."

God is no respecter of persons ; the weakest in *natural* powers are sometimes endowed the most richly with *spiritual* gifts.

"It is by being often upon our knees, by reiterating our prayers, by shewing God that we feel the value of faith, and by adding to prayer the exercise of it, that we receive in answer to a first prayer a little faith, by which we are encouraged to more fervent prayer, which will again obtain a new measure of it, that we shall attain to the full measure of faith.

" To grow in faith, we have three things to do : to ask it, to exercise it, and to contemplate examples of it in the great saints, by a deep study of the Scriptures. We must not hope to obtain anything from God if we do not feel the value of it."*

How is it that in the present day there is so much worldly conformity, even among the Lord's own people ? How is it that the line of separation between the world and the church, instead of being clear, broad, and unmistakable, is so faint, so undefined, that it can hardly be perceived ? How is it that believers are not more earnestly desirous, not only for the growth and healthy condition of their own souls, but to be the means of bringing others to Jesus ? Because fa th has

* Adolphe Monod

C

decreased so grievously, that in the
hearts of many it has dwindled to a
mere speck. What need have we, in deep
self-abasement, to offer unceasingly the
apostle's prayer, " Lord, increase our
faith !" By faith alone can we " come
out and be separate" from the world; by
faith alone can we realise that we are
already "risen with Christ." "*Little* faith
will bring the soul to heaven, but *great*
faith will bring heaven into the soul."*

Believer, it is your privilege *now*, at
this *present moment*, to dwell above, to
abide in the heart of Jesus—"Whom
having not seen, ye love; in whom,
though now ye see him not, yet believing, ye rejoice with joy unspeakable and
full of glory. Receiving the end of your
faith, even the salvation of *your souls*."

* Life of Mrs Mary Winslow.

" Faith is a precious grace,
   Where'er it is bestow'd ;
It boasts of a celestial birth,
   And is the gift of God.

" Jesus it owns as King,
   And all-atoning Priest ;
It claims no merit of its own,
   But looks for all in Christ.

" To Him it leads the soul,
   When fill'd with deep distress,
Flees to the fountain of His blood,
   And trusts His righteousness.

" All through the wilderness,
   It is our strength and stay ;
Nor can we miss the heavenly road,
   If faith direct our way.

" Lord, 'tis Thy work alone,
   And that divinely free ;
Send down the Spirit of Thy Son, .
   To work this faith in me."

CHAPTER IV.

𝔖𝔲𝔟𝔪𝔦𝔰𝔰𝔦𝔬𝔫.

" He was oppressed, and he was afflicted, yet he opened not his mouth: he is brought as a lamb to the slaughter, and as a sheep before her shearers is dumb, so he openeth not his mouth."—ISA. liii. 7.

" Father, if thou be willing, remove this cup from me: nevertheless, not my will, but thine, be done."—LUKE xxii. 42.

"Christ also suffered for us, leaving us an example, that ye should follow his steps."—1 PET. ii. 21.

" Submit yourselves therefore to God."—JAMES iv. 7.

"Humble yourselves therefore under the mighty hand of God, that he may exalt you in due time."—1 PET. v. 6.

"Take, my brethren, the prophets, who have spoken in the name of the Lord, for an example of suffering affliction, and of patience. Behold, we count them happy which endure. Ye have heard of the patience of Job, and have seen the end of the Lord; that the Lord is very pitiful, and of tender mercy."—JAMES v. 10, 11.

"And Aaron held his peace."—LEV. x. 3.

"Run now, I pray thee, to meet her, and say unto her, Is it well with thee? is it well with thy husband? is it well with the child? And she answered, It is well."—2 KINGS iv. 26.

"Thy will be done."—LUKE xi. 2.

" It is Thy hand, my God!
    My sorrow comes from Thee;
I bow beneath Thy chast'ning rod;
    'Tis love that bruises me.

" I would not murmur, Lord,
    Before Thee I am dumb;
Lest I should breathe one murmuring word,
    To Thee for help I come.

" My God, Thy name is love,
    A Father's hand is thine;
With tearful eyes I look above,
    And cry, ' Thy will be mine.'

" I know Thy will is right,
    Though it may seem severe;
Thy path is still unsullied light,
    Though dark it oft appear.

" Jesus for me hath died;
    Thy Son Thou didst not spare;
His piercèd hands, His bleeding side,
    Thy love for me declare.

" Here my poor heart can rest,
    My God, it cleaves to Thee:
Thy will is love, Thy end is blest,
    All work for good to me."

"IT is well." Such was the reply of the Shunammite to the prophet's inquiry, "Is it well with thee? is it well with thy husband? is it well with the child?" She had just closed the eyes of her first-born, the child for whom she had waited so many years. No other little ones claimed her loving attention, and thus prevented her from indulging the full tide of her grief. He was her *only* one; "beside him she had neither son nor daughter." In him was centred the whole of a fond mother's affection.

"Her life was bound up in the lad's life." And yet, when the stroke had just fallen upon her, and her very soul was writhing under its severity, she was enabled to say in the meek submission of faith, "It is well." *Well*, though the desire of her eyes had been suddenly torn from her embrace. *Weil*, even while her fainting heart was realising the full bitterness of sorrow. From one source alone could the Shunammite have learned her lesson of meek resignation.

Her intercourse with the prophet had not been in vain. While ministering to his wants, she had imbibed his spirit. From him she had learned to trust in the God of Israel. She had esteemed it a privilege to receive him into her house, and to "wash his feet," for in this "holy man of God" she discerned the likeness of his Master.

A time had now arrived when she was called upon to prove the *sincerity* of her faith. As in the case of Abraham, the Lord claimed the object that lay nearest to her heart; He smote her in the tenderest part, till every fibre trembled beneath the stroke.

Had her child been an idol?

Scripture does not supply an answer to this question; but it is possible that she had been too much engrossed with this beloved object of her affection, that she needed some reminder to teach her that even the pure devotion of a mother might become idolatrous. Be this as it may, her heavenly Father saw that the chastisement was needful, and, strong in faith, she at once recognised His hand in the blow, and meekly bowed to His will.

There is a touching calmness in the martyr-like submission of this bereaved mother,—a calmness which could only proceed from a renewed and sanctified heart. Without *divine* support, the Shunammite would have been rebellious and impatient as another; but she had learned to trust in Jehovah alone : hence the strength which firmly supported her in the hour of trial. In Elisha (a singularly striking type of the Lord Jesus) she recognised the only individual to whom she could look for help and comfort. He had been the means of "guiding her feet into the way of peace," and to him she now turns for sympathy. She does not even make her husband acquainted with their common bereavement, but goes at once to the prophet, feeling that he alone can enter into the depth of her sorrow. She needs more than *earthly* comfort, and, guided by the partial light then vouchsafed to the believing Israelite, applies to the only source from whence she can obtain it.

In the simple trust of the Shunammite may be traced the same faith which, in the time of trial, guides the believer to his Saviour. How instinctively does the true child of God, when visited by afflic-tion, turn at once to Jesus, feeling that He alone is able to deliver and support him,—that He alone can subdue the rebellious will, and impart that genuine submission which enables him calmly and truthfully to say, " It is well."

" O precious Saviour! Thou hast passed through the *depths* of affliction,

Thou hast known the *extremity* of suffering. Thy Father's face hidden from Thee, the powers of hell let loose upon Thy spotless soul,—'was any sorrow like unto *Thy* sorrow?' And yet, amidst the agonies of Gethsemane and the pangs of the cross, ' Father, not my will, but Thine be done,' was Thine ever-ascending prayer. Oh, teach Thy children the same lesson of submissive love, that the world may see and acknowledge their likeness to a crucified Saviour." Wherever *genuine* submission is exercised by an afflicted saint, it must be accompanied by the persuasion that the chastisement is sent by a God of *love*, who " doth not *willingly* afflict" His chosen ones, but who chastens them " for their profit, that they may be partakers of His holiness." Calmly resting upon this truth, as upon an immovable rock, the believer finds sweetness in the bitterest cup, since it is administered by the love of his covenant God. And, O precious truth! he feels that he is not left to bear his burden alone, since every pang touches a chord in his Redeemer's heart, and brings back an answer of sympathy.

> " In every pang that rends the heart
>   The Man of sorrows bears a part,
>   And still remembers in the skies
>   His tears, and groans, and agonies."

Who can fathom the depth of love which the Saviour bears to His people? " In all their afflictions He is afflicted ;" " Whoso toucheth them toucheth the apple of His eye;" and—mysterious but blessed truth!—they are so completely a part of Himself, as to be blended into His very being: "We are members of his body, of his flesh, and of his bones," (Eph. v. 30.)

The knowledge of his indissoluble union with the Saviour is not only the *comfort*, but the *strength* of the believer. In *himself* he has no power either to bear (with patience and meekness) the daily crossing of his own inclinations, or the crushing trial which "bows his head as a bulrush."

Daily, nay, *hourly*, does he experience the inward rising of rebellion and self-will, although, at the same time, he may pray in truthful earnestness,—

> " *Subdue* my will from day to day,
> Blend it with Thine, and take away
> All that now makes it hard to say,
> ' Thy will be done.'"

He feels that his only strength, his only safety, lies in his Saviour, and that *abiding* in Him, the *fulness* of Jesus is placed at his disposal. *Nothing* in ourselves—without the power to produce or to exercise one Christian grace—" in the Lord *alone* have we righteousness and strength." And oh, the comfort, the joy of *knowing*, of *believing*, that *all* is *well*,—that the sharpest stroke, the darkest dispensation, is a link in the golden chain of the Lord's providential dealings with us. The *richest* consolations are sent in the hour of deepest trial. *Then* we learn the *depth*, the *intensity* of our Redeemer's love; we feel its *reality*, we *rest* upon it, and *live* upon it. We are assured that our Father would not send us one needless pang. We look forward, and feel that "as the Captain of our salvation was made perfect through suffering," so the Lord is purifying *us* in the "furnace of affliction," that thereby we may be ripened for glory. In this assurance we rest, and are enabled in faith and hope to "*rejoice* in tribulation," believing assuredly that "*all* things work together for good to them that love God."

> " Through the love of God our Saviour,
>   All will be well;
>   Free and changeless is His favour,—
>   All will be well.
>   Precious is the blood that heal'd us,
>   Perfect is the grace that seal'd us,
>   Strong the hand stretch'd forth to shield us,—
>   All *must* be well.
>
> " Though we pass through tribulation,
>   All will be well;
>   Ours is such a full salvation,
>   All, all is well.

Happy, whilst in God confiding,
Fruitful, whilst in Christ abiding,
Holy, by the Spirit's guiding,
    All must be well.

" We expect a bright to-morrow,—
    All will be well ;
Faith can sing through days of sorrow,
    All, all is well.
On that changeless love relying,
Which our need is still supplying,
Or in living or in dying,
    All will be well."

CHAPTER V.

𝕹ot 𝕹ow.

"And when Jesus was come into the ship, he that had been possessed with the devil prayed him that he might be with him. Howbeit Jesus suffered him not, but saith unto him, Go home to thy friends, and tell them how great things the Lord hath done for thee, and hath had compassion on thee. And he departed, and began to publish in Decapolis how great things Jesus had done for him, and all men did marvel."—MARK v. 18-20.

"For the Son of man is as a man taking a far journey, who left his house, and gave authority to his servants, and *to every man his work*, and commanded the porter to watch."—MARK xiii. 34.

"Son, go work to-day in my vineyard."—MATT. xxi. 28.

"As every man hath received the gift, even so minister the same one to another, as good stewards of the manifold grace of God."—1 PETER iv. 10.

"They that be wise [or, teachers] shall shine as the brightness of the firmament, and they that turn many to righteousness as the stars for ever and ever."—DAN. xii. 3.

" Not *now*, my child,—a little more rough tossing,
  A little longer on the billows' foam,
A few more journeyings in the desert-darkness,
  And *then* the sunshine of thy Father's home !

" Not *now*,—for I have wanderers in the distance,
  And thou must call them in with patient love ;
Not *now*,—for I have sheep upon the mountains,
  And thou must follow them where'er they rove.

" Not *now*,—for I have loved ones sad and weary,
  Wilt thou not cheer them with a kindly smile ?
Sick ones who need thee in their lonely sorrow,
  Wilt thou not tend them yet a little while ?

" Not *now*,—for wounded hearts are sorely bleeding,
  And thou must teach these widow'd hearts to sing ;
Not *now*,—for orphans' tears are thickly falling,
  They must be gathered 'neath some sheltering wing.

" Not *now*,—for many a hungry one is pining,
  Thy willing hand must be outstretch'd and free,
Thy Father hears the mighty cry of anguish ;
  And gives His answering messages to thee.

" Not *now*,—for dungeon walls look stern and gloomy,
  And prisoners' sighs sound strangely on the breeze,—
Man's prisoners, but thy Saviour's noble freemen ;
  Hast Thou no ministry of love for these ?

" Not *now*,—for hell's eternal gulf is yawning,
  And souls are perishing in hopeless sin ;
Jerusalem's bright gates are standing open,—
  Go to the banish'd ones, and fetch them in.

" Go with the name of Jesus to the dying,
  And speak that name in all its living power,
Why should thy fainting heart grow chill and weary ;
  Canst thou not *watch with me* one little hour ?

" One little hour !—and *then* the glorious crowning,
  The golden harp-strings and the victor's palm,—
One little hour !—and *then* the hallelujah !
  Eternity's long, deep thanksgiving psalm !"

                                          C. P.

"AND they come to Jesus, and see him that was possessed with the devil, and had the legion, sitting, and clothed, and in his right mind."

A little while before, and he was wandering naked among the mountains, dwelling with the dead, possessed not with *one* only, but "*many* devils." But Jesus had spoken, and at His word Satan and his legion had been compelled to flee, and, no longer under their dominion, the once raging maniac had become gentle as a little child. What wonder that, in the first hour of restoration, his whole heart should flow forth in love to his Deliverer, and that in a transport of gratitude he should pray to be always with Him ? By the side of Jesus he felt that there was safety and rest. He had just witnessed the power of His word, in delivering him instantaneously from the unclean spirits, who had held him in cruel bondage for so many years; and the same voice, calm as a flowing rill, had entered into the depths of his own soul, restoring his reason, and introducing order and peace, where before all was tumult and confusion. The true child of God can fully enter into every particular of this thrilling narrative, feeling, as he does, that the whole is a faithful picture of his own condition, when, as a lost and guilty sinner, Jesus sought and saved him.

He remembers the warmth of his "first love," the tenderness of his renewed spirit, when, in the rapturous language of the heavenly bride, he could say, "My Beloved is mine, and I am His." He recollects his ardent longing to be "for ever with the Lord," his utter distaste for the pleasures and pursuits of the world, and his secret fear, lest, with a long pilgrimage still before him, his heart should grow cold towards his Saviour, and turn again to the flesh-pots of Egypt. As memory thus recalls the past, it awakens a fellow-feeling for the restored lunatic, and the Christian, for a moment, is disposed to wonder that the Saviour does not at *once* grant his request. And was the gracious Redeemer unmindful of His child's love? Oh no! Listen to the language in

which he addresses His Church (composed, be it remembered, of pardoned
sinners, to whom, in their natural state,
the poor Gadarene bears but a faint resemblance :)—"How fair is thy love, my
sister, my spouse !   How much better is
thy love than wine, and the smell of thine
ointment than all spices !"   Precious in
the sight of Jesus is the love of His
people. The first prayer of His restored
one was as music in His ear, far sweeter
than to a mother is the wail of her new-
born infant.   Who can measure the love
of Christ to His chosen ones ? So *deep*,
that it cannot be fathomed. So *faithful*,
that it cannot change. So *wise*, that it
cannot err. His child longs to be always with Him, to "go no more out."
He *knows*, he *feels* that he is saved, and
with this he is satisfied. But his Lord

has other views for him. His will is not
only that he should be saved *himself*,
but that he should be the means of
bringing other sheep to the fold. His
will is, that in glory he may wear a
starry crown, and have a " full reward ;"
therefore, " Jesus suffered him not, but
saith unto him, Go home to thy friends,
and *tell them* how great things the Lord
hath done for thee, and hath had compassion on thee."

O believer! art *thou* resting satisfied
with thine own salvation, making no
effort for the Lord's glory in the salvation of others ? Has thy Master no
work for *thee?* Are there no lost
sheep to be followed, and " guided into
the way of peace ?" no sorrowing saints
to be comforted ? no children to be
" brought up in the nurture and ad-

monition of the Lord?" Is there no "work of faith and labour of love," whereby thou mayst shew thy gratitude to Him who has done so much for thee? *Remember* that the Son of man giveth "to *every man* his work." There is some *special* work for thee, which thou alone canst execute. Thou mayst feel thyself but a feeble instrument, and thy work may be a lowly, unostentatious one; but not less, on that account, to thy Lord's glory, for "God hath chosen the foolish things of the world to confound the things which are mighty; and base things of the world, and things which are despised, hath God chosen, yea, and things that are not, to bring to nought things that are, that no flesh should glory in his presence," (1 Cor. i. 27–29.) Every saint, whatever be his station, whether he be high or low, learned or unlearned, has a double mission to perform. His Lord sends him, as He did the restored Gadarene, on a mission of mercy to the unconverted around him,—to his relations, his friends, his neighbours, all who are still in the darkness and captivity of sin. "Tell them," He says, "how great things the Lord hath done for *thee*, and hath had compassion on *thee*." "Go out into the streets and lanes of the city, and bring in hither the poor, and the maimed, and the halt, and the blind."

The believer has also a ministry of love among his fellow-Christians. He has his own distinct place and office in the body of Christ; and if his ap-

pointed work be neglected, not only
will his sloth and carelessness bring
guilt and leanness on his *own* soul, but
his fellow-members will suffer. In
Eph. iv. 16, we are told that the "whole
body, fitly joined together and com-
pacted by that which *every joint sup-
plieth*, according to the *effectual working*
in the measure of every part, maketh
increase of the body unto the edifying
of itself in love." Charity, or love, is
called by the apostle Paul "the *bond* of
perfectness;" therefore the love mani-
fested by each believer is the bond
which unites every individual member
of the Lord's body into one symmet-
rical whole.

This love, which flows from the Lord
Jesus alone, the great Head of the mystical body, discovers itself in all those

nameless offices of Christian kindness
and sympathy which the true believer
delights to exercise towards his fellow-
members. Every day, every hour, he
feels the deep debt of gratitude and
love which he owes to his Redeemer;
and as that Redeemer has said, "Inasmuch as ye have done it unto the
least of these my brethren, ye have
done it unto me," his heart warms
towards those in whom he traces the
image of his Lord, and he feels it his
highest privilege to minister to their
wants, to sympathise in their sorrows,
and to prove by his love to *them* his
devotion to his adorable Master.

" Sweet is the union true believers feel;
  Into one spirit they have drunk; the seal
  Of God is in their hearts; and thus they see
  In each the features of one family.

"If one is suffering, all the rest are sad;
  If but the least is honour'd, all are glad;
  The grace of Jesus, which they all partake,
  Flows out in mutual kindness for His sake.

"Here He has left them for a while to wait,
  And represent Him in His suffering state;
  While He, their Head, yet glorified alone,
  Bears the whole Church before the Father's throne."

CHAPTER VI.

The Wilderness.

"Who is this that cometh up from the wilderness, leaning upon her beloved?"—CANT. viii. 5.

"He found him in a desert land, and in the waste howling wilderness; he led him about, he instructed him, he kept him as the apple of his eye. As an eagle stirreth up her nest, fluttereth over her young, spreadeth abroad her wings, taketh them, beareth them on her wings: so the Lord alone did lead him, and there was no strange god with him."—DEUT. xxxii. 10-12.

"Therefore, behold, I will allure her, and bring her into the wilderness, and speak comfortably unto her."—HOS. ii. 14.

"And he said unto them, Come ye yourselves apart into a desert place, and rest a while: for there were many coming and going, and they had no leisure so much as to eat."—MARK vi. 31.

"He made his own people to go forth like sheep, and guided them in the wilderness like a flock"—PSALM lxxviii. 52.

"And thou shalt remember all the way which the Lord thy God led thee these forty years in the wilderness, to humble thee, and to prove thee, to know what was in thine heart, whether thou wouldest keep his commandments, or no."—DEUT. viii. 2.

" Rise, my soul, thy God directs thee,
 Stranger hands no more impede ;
Pass thou on, His hand protects thee,
 Strength that has the captive freed.

" Is the wilderness before thee—
 Desert lands where drought abides ?
Heavenly springs shall there restore thee,
 Fresh from God's exhaustless tides.

" Light divine surrounds thy going,
 God himself shall mark thy way ;
Secret blessings richly flowing,
 Lead to everlasting day.

" In the desert God will teach thee
 What the God that thou hast found—
Patient, gracious, powerful, holy,
 All His grace shall there abound.

" Though thy way be long and dreary,
 Eagle strength He'll still renew ;
Garments fresh and feet unweary
 Tell how God hath brought thee through.

" When to Canaan's long-loved dwelling,
 Love divine thy foot shall bring,
There, with shouts of triumph swelling,
 Zion's songs in rest to sing,—

" There no stranger-god shall meet thee,
 Stranger thou in courts above ;
He who to His rest shall greet thee,
 Greets thee with a well-known love."

THE Wilderness! What a familiar name is this to the Lord's people! It speaks to them of dangers and deliverances, of failure and discipline, of wanderings and restorations. It is a word which comes home to their hearts, recalling their own waywardness and folly, and a Saviour's changeless, ever-enduring love. They delight to dwell upon its bygone scenes, some sad and painful, some bright and joyous, but all alike reminding them of a Father's loving-

E

kindness and tender mercy. God frequently makes use of trial as a means
of bringing the sinner to himself. How
many saved ones "found grace in the
wilderness!" (Jer. xxxi. 2.) How many
in the time of affliction, when all around
was dark and dreary, when the future
was shrouded in gloom, and the soul
was desolate and dismayed, listened for
the first time to the gracious invitation
of Jesus, "Come unto me, all ye that
labour and are heavy laden, and I will
give you rest!" Various are the trials
which the Lord employs in bringing
sinners to Himself. Sickness, adversity,
bereavement, disappointed schemes,
blighted hopes, these are among the
countless modes by which He works
His sovereign purpose, making "His
people willing in the day of His power."

And when the eternal word has gone forth, when His time to save a soul has fully come, who "can stay His hand, or say unto Him, What doest thou?" Then the hard heart grows soft, the rebel will is broken, and the first trembling prayer ascends to heaven, "God be merciful to me a sinner." The soul is brought into the wilderness to be alone with Jesus. Alone with Him, to listen with an undistracted mind, with an undivided heart, to the wondrous tale of His love and mercy. "I will allure her, and bring her into the wilderness, and speak comfortably unto her,"—literally, *to her heart.* And oh, how sweetly, how soothingly does the voice of Jesus come home to the heart of the awakened sinner, telling him of rest and peace for his weary, sin-burdened soul!

" I heard the voice of Jesus say,
  ' Come unto me, and rest ;
Lay down, thou weary one, lay down
  Thy head upon my breast.'
I came to Jesus as I was,
  Weary, and worn, and sad ;
I found in Him a resting-place,
  And He has made me glad."

Truly to the restored wanderer, the wilderness, with all its sterility, all its isolation, is a place of sweet and holy memories, since it was *there* that his Lord "found him," *there* that he learned "to know the love of Christ," *there* that his Saviour delivered him from death, and made him a partaker of everlasting life.

But the pardoned sinner's first introduction to the wilderness is but the beginning of desert-life. He has many a lesson to learn, many a trial to undergo, before his pilgrimage is ended. "The

Lord found him in a desert land, and in the waste howling wilderness; he led him about, he instructed him, he kept him as the apple of his eye." How incessant, how unwearied is the care which our heavenly Father bestows upon His children! "His way is *perfect.*" He can make no mistakes. The best, the tenderest of earthly parents are liable to err. Their very *love* may become a snare, blinding their judgment, and misdirecting their wisest efforts. But the Lord's dealings with His people are *perfect* in wisdom, *perfect* in love. With one end in view, their eternal happiness, all the discipline, all the training, which each adopted child undergoes, is but making him "meet for the inheritance of the saints in light." Without it he would not be fitted for the full enjoy-

ment of "the things which God hath
prepared for them that love Him." The
painful bereavement, the bitter cup of
adversity, the wearing sickness, is wean-
ing him from the things of this world,
and making him *realise* their emptiness
and vanity; it is calling forth and ex-
ercising those Christian graces which
before were drooping and inactive; it
is constraining him to set his heart and
affections more entirely upon things
above.

Wilderness-discipline is also a fre-
quent preparation for some peculiar
sphere of labour in the Lord's vineyard.
Thus Joseph, from his tedious imprison-
ment, came forth as the deliverer of
Egypt, and the saviour of his brethren.
Moses, during his long sojourn in the
wilderness, was preparing to come before

Pharaoh as the champion and leader of
God's chosen people. John the Baptist
"was in the deserts till the day of his
shewing unto Israel;" and our blessed
Lord himself "was led up of the Spirit
into the wilderness to be tempted of the
devil," before He entered upon His public course of ministry. How needful is
this wilderness-preparation for future
usefulness! Alone with God, the soul
learns its own emptiness, and at the
same time the fulness of Jesus. It discovers that, though destitute of all resources in itself, the spiritual supplies
laid up in Christ are boundless and
inexhaustible; that, resting wholly on
Him, there is no work too vast, no labour
too great, for faith to undertake and accomplish. Thus, "strong in the Lord,
and in the power of His might," it goes

forth from its seclusion, as the stripling David to meet Goliath, confident of success, because resting on God alone.

But God has another end in view, in thus drawing His people aside for a season. He sees that they need retirement; that in the busy scene of public life (even *Christian* life) they are in danger of neglecting their own *personal* communion with Jesus. And *nothing* will make up for this. We may be actively employed for the good of others, we may be "instant in season and out of season," we may be wearing our strength away in the public service of God, and yet our *own* souls may be lean and impoverished. "They made me keeper of the vineyards; but mine *own* vineyard have I not kept."

If *private* prayer be short and hurried,

if there be little or no time for the study
of God's Word, and for calm undisturbed intercourse with Christ, the soul
can neither be healthy or thriving.

"And Jesus said unto them, Come ye
yourselves apart into a desert place, and
rest a while; for there were many coming
and going, and they had no leisure so
much as to eat."

How gracious and tender is the
Saviour's care for His disciples! They
had just returned from a mission upon
which their Lord had sent them. They
were no doubt weary and hungry.
They had been ministering to others,
employed in the Master's work; and now,
in His loving thoughtfulness, He takes
them aside for a time, that their *own*
wants may be attended to.

O believer! repine not at the tem-

porary ailment which for a few hours
calls thee away from active life, or at the
protracted illness which lays thee aside
even for weeks or months.   It is but the
gentle loving voice of thy Saviour, saying unto thee, " Come apart into a desert
place, and rest a while."   Rather pray
that the season of loneliness may be a
blessed interval of repose—of undisturbed communion with the Beloved.
"And then shalt thou *remember* all the
way which the Lord thy God led thee
these forty years in the wilderness, to
humble thee, and to prove thee, to know
.what was in thine heart, whether thou
wouldest keep his commandments, or
no."   It is a good thing to *retrace* our
wilderness-life, to recall the past, and
remember how the good hand of our
God has been with us throughout our

desert-wanderings, guiding us, chastening us, and upholding us.

Such recollections of spiritual joys and
deliverances, of conflicts and victories,
are so many altar stones, upon which
the believing soul loves to dwell, not
only to praise God for the past, but to
take courage for the future. Thus David
encouraged himself by the Lord's past
dealings with him. "O my God, my
soul is cast down within me: *therefore*
will I *remember* thee from the land of
Jordan, and of the Hermonites, from
the hill Mizar," (Ps. xlii. 6.) Thus
Abraham "called on the name of the
Lord," in "the place of the altar, which
he had made there at the first."

Soon, very soon, our desert-life, with
all its fluctuations, its chequered path
of joys and sorrows, dangers and de-

liverances, will be over, and we shall have reached our eternal home. Oh that while *still* in the midst of our pilgrimage, still experiencing its vicissitudes, and surrounded by its temptations, we may be kept "leaning on our Beloved," *dwelling* at His side, *abiding* in His love! Thus shall our sojourn here be joy and peace, and "an entrance be ministered unto us abundantly into the everlasting kingdom of our Lord and Saviour Jesus Christ."

"Blest wilderness! where first my soul
Waked to perceive my life's true goal;
Blest wilderness! that made me prove
A Saviour's power—a Father's love;
Where the world's din died on my ear,
That I in secret God might hear;
Amidst whose scenes of solemn truth
Faded the fair false dreams of youth.
Ne'er had I learn'd God's power to bless,
Had I not known—the wilderness.

Dark is the scene to Nature's eye,
A dreary waste, unblest and dry,
Where I must thread my lonely way,
'Mid rocks, and snares, and beasts of prey.
Gloomy that barren plain, 'tis true,
Yet arch'd with Heaven's own cloudless blue.
What though no cultured spots be given,
My daily bread comes down from heaven.
When, faint with thirst, a stream I see,
Unseal'd by God's own hand for me ;
While Faith, on this low barren ground,
Brings glorious Canaan smiling round,
Joy strangely mingles with distress,
Such prospects light the wilderness.
Thus be my journey till I come
Rejoicing to my Father's home ;
Throughout eternity to bless
My Saviour for—the wilderness !"

CHAPTER VII.

Separation from the World.

"Wherefore come out from among them, and be ye separate, saith the Lord, and touch not the unclean thing; and I will receive you, and will be a Father unto you, and ye shall be my sons and daughters, saith the Lord Almighty."—2 Cor. vi. 17, 18.

"Having therefore these promises, dearly beloved, let us cleanse ourselves from all filthiness of the flesh and spirit, perfecting holiness in the fear of God."—2 Cor. vii. 1.

"And be not conformed to this world : but be ye transformed by the renewing of your mind, that ye may prove what is that good, and acceptable, and perfect will of God."—Rom. xii. 2.

"Love not the world, neither the things that are in the world. If any man love the world, the love of the Father is not in him. For all that is in the world, the lust of the flesh, and the lust of the eyes, and the pride of life, is not of the Father, but is of the world."—1 John ii. 15, 16.

"Grace be to you and peace from God the Father, and from our Lord Jesus Christ, who gave himself for our sins, that he might deliver us from this present evil world, according to the will of God and our Father: to whom be glory for ever and ever. Amen."—Gal. i. 3-5.

"A child of God! and can this earth's vain pleasures
    Be aught to one for whom the Saviour died?
Rise! rise above them all! its worthless treasures,
    Its soul-destroying joys, its pomp and pride.
Be His in all! thy soul and eye be single,
    Fix'd on the glory that surrounds the throne;
Seek not Christ's service with the world's to mingle,
    Remember God hath seal'd thee for His own."

N studying the history of God's chosen people Israel, it is impossible not to be struck with the fact, that in spite of the Lord's repeated warnings, they continually brought themselves into sin and trouble by "mingling with the heathen." They were solemnly commanded to have no intercourse with them, to make no marriages with them, to enter into no covenant with them, to conform to none of their customs, and to walk in none of their ordinances, and this because God had "chosen Israel to be a peculiar treasure unto Himself." They were to be a separate and distinct nation, a "holy and special people," a "kingdom of priests." "Now therefore, if ye will obey my voice indeed, and keep my covenant, then ye shall be a peculiar treasure unto me above all people : for all the earth is mine. And ye shall be unto me a kingdom of priests, and an holy nation," (Exod. xix. 5, 6.) "And ye shall be holy unto me, for I the Lord am holy, and have severed you from other people, that ye should be mine," (Lev. xx. 26.) Through the whole of their wilderness-journey we find the children of Israel continually falling into sin, and incurring the anger and punishment of God, by their unholy alliances with heathen nations. We are told that, when they left Egypt, "a

mixt multitude went up also with them."
These were not pure Israelites, but were
probably composed of Egyptians, who
followed them from motives of interest
or worldly attachment. In Num. xi. 4
we find that this "mixt multitude fell a-
lusting," (longing after the dainties of
Egypt,) and, drawing the Israelites into
the same sin, "the wrath of God came
upon them, and slew the fattest of them,
and smote down the chosen men of
Israel," (Ps. lxxviii. 31.) Again, in
Judges iii. 5–8, we read, "And the
children of Israel dwelt among the
Canaanites, Hittites, and Amorites, and
Perizzites, and Hivites, and Jebusites:
and they took their daughters to be
their wives, and gave their daughters to
their sons, and served their gods. And
the children of Israel did evil in the

sight of the Lord, and forgat the Lord
their God, and served Baalim and the
groves. Therefore the anger of the Lord
was hot against Israel: and he sold
them into the hand of Chushan-risha-
thaim, king of Mesopotamia."

In Israel of old we behold a type of
the Church—of those redeemed ones,
whom the Lord Jesus hath purchased
with His own blood. They, too, "are
a chosen generation, a royal priesthood,
a holy nation, a peculiar people." *Taken
out* of the world, to form a bride for the
Saviour, how exalted is their position!
how glorious their destiny! They are
"espoused to one husband," even to
Christ. He has bought them to be His
own, to be sacred to Himself. And, O
wondrous truth! He is jealous of their
love; He will not share it with another;

He must have their undivided heart.
Wonder of wonders! that the Lord of
glory should thus set His love upon
fallen man, the wreck of creation, and,
lifting him out of his misery and ruin,
should make him a part of Himself, the
sharer of His eternal glory! Not less
wonderful, that any thus redeemed and
set apart for Jesus should suffer themselves to be again entangled and drawn
aside by the world which crucified their
Lord.

But, alas! is it not so? Is not the
world in its varied forms of fascination
and pleasure continually insinuating
itself into the hearts even of true believers? Is not the worldly conformity
of the present day a deadly evil in the
Church of God? Does she not impair
her power, weaken her influence, and

bring dishonour upon her Lord, by weakly and sinfully conforming to worldly customs, worldly fashions, and worldly principles? How emphatic, how unmistakable, is the warning word, "Come out from among them, and be ye separate, saith the Lord, and touch not the unclean thing." The world *is* an unclean thing to the believer. He cannot touch it without being defiled. Its fashions, its pleasures, its books, its pursuits, *all, all* bear the brand of iniquity, the taint of sin. And shall the bride of Jesus allow herself to be seduced by this uncircumcised stranger? Shall she leave the side of her Lord to embrace His enemy? Shall she suffer the robes which have been "washed and made white in the blood of the Lamb," to become spotted

by unholy intercourse with Mammon?
No! By the agonies of Gethsemane,
by the memory of Calvary, by the dying
love of her crucified Lord, let her rather
wrap the vail of widowhood around her,
and mourn the long delay of Him who
gave His life for her ransom.

Surely, in the absence of the Bridegroom, it is more comely for the bride
to be "sitting alone" than whiling away
the interval by "pleasing herself with
the children of strangers." Oh that
"the Church of the living God, the
pillar and ground of the truth," may,
through the power of the Holy Ghost,
realise her true position as the representative of Jesus, the light of the
world, the salt of the earth, and, instead of descending into worldly life
and mixing with the ungodly, take up

her *abode* where it is her *privilege* ever
to dwell, "in heavenly places in Christ
Jesus." Thus will her influence be felt
and acknowledged even by those who
may smile at her singularity; thus will
she be a "living epistle, known and
read of all men;" thus will she be faith-
fully fulfilling her Lord's commission,
"Let your light so shine before men,
that they may see your good works,
and glorify your Father which is in
heaven."

O believer! is the world in any
form taking hold of thy heart and affections, and drawing them away from
Jesus? Is it engrossing the time, the
influence, the talent which ought to be
devoted to thy Lord's glory? If so,
thou art but a half-hearted disciple, a
lukewarm servant,—unfaithful to thy

Master, unfaithful to thine own soul,
unfaithful to 'thy fellow-Christians.
" Know ye not that the friendship
of the world is enmity with God ?
Whosoever therefore will be a friend
of the world is the enemy of God."
Surely this declaration should make
the worldly Christian tremble, should
lead to deep self-abasement and solemn
searching of heart, that he may be enabled by God's grace to cast out the
accursed thing, which hinders him from
serving God, destroys the joy and
peace of his own soul, and prevents
his being made a blessing either to the
unconverted or to his fellow-believers.
It has been truly said, that " God will
not use an unclean vessel ;" and if His
people defile themselves by unhallowed
intercourse with the world, they cannot

be "vessels *meet* for the Master's use."
If the believer would labour *successfully*
in the Lord's service; if his desire is
to be a *faithful* steward during his
Master's absence; if in the great day
of reckoning he would secure a "full
reward," and gain an "abundant entrance" into the kingdom of glory, let
him prayerfully and resolutely repel the
advances of that insidious foe, whose
presence is contamination, and whose
embrace is death.

"Again with increased earnestness
we beseech you, love not the world,
imitate not the world, go not needlessly
into the world! It is a cruel, treacher-
ous, soul-destroying world. It crucified
your Lord, and seeks nothing less than
your eternal destruction. Come out of
it, and let your unearthly principles,

and holy enjoyments, and heavenly-
mindedness, and simplicity of walk, in-
tegrity and uprightness in all your trans-
actions with the world, be a witness
against it for God, for Christ, for eternity. Labour for its good, pray for it,
and if need be suffer for it ; but let your
daily motto be,—the mark of Christ
upon your forehead,—'God forbid that
I should glory, save in the cross of our
Lord Jesus Christ, by whom the world
is crucified unto me, and I unto the
world.'"*

" How long, O Lord our Saviour,
   Wilt Thou remain away?
Our hearts are growing weary
   Of Thy so long delay.
Oh, when shall come the moment
   When, brighter far than morn,
The sunshine of Thy glory
   Shall on Thy people dawn?

* The Inner Life, by Dr Winslow.

" How long, O gracious Master,
  Wilt Thou Thy household leave ?
So long hast Thou now tarried,
  Few Thy return believe.
Immersed in sloth and folly,
  Thy servants, Lord, we see;
And few of us stand ready
  With joy to welcome Thee.

" How long, O heavenly Bridegroom,
  How long wilt Thou delay ?
And yet how few are grieving
  That Thou dost absent stay !
Thy very bride her portion
  And calling hath forgot,
And seeks for ease and glory
  Where Thou her Lord art not.

" Oh, wake Thy slumbering virgins !
  Send forth the solemn cry,—
Let all Thy saints repeat it,—
  ' The Bridegroom draweth nigh!'
May all our lamps be burning,
  Our loins well girded be,
Each longing heart preparing
  With joy Thy face to see !"

CHAPTER VIII.

Chastisement.

"Thou shalt also consider in thine heart, that, as a man chasteneth his son, so the Lord thy God chasteneth thee."—DEUT. viii. 5.

"Whom the Lord loveth he chasteneth, and scourgeth every son whom he receiveth."—HEB. xii. 6.

"Blessed is the man whom thou chastenest, O Lord, and teachest him out of thy law."—PSALM xciv. 12.

"Behold, happy is the man whom God correcteth : therefore despise not thou the chastening of the Almighty."—JOB v. 17.

"As many as I love, I rebuke and chasten."—REV. iii. 19.

"Now no chastening for the present seemeth to be joyous, but grievous : nevertheless afterward it yieldeth the peaceable fruit of righteousness unto them which are exercised thereby."—HEB. xii. 11.

"Now for a season, if need be, ye are in heaviness through manifold temptations : that the trial of your faith, being much more precious than of gold that perisheth, though it be tried with fire, might be found unto praise and honour and glory at the appearing of Jesus Christ."—1 PET. i. 6, 7.

" Welcome thy gentle scourge ! Thou precious Lord,
Small are the cords Thy love hath intertwined,
And light the stroke.   I own the just award
Of strife, when in Thy temple Thou dost find
Unmeet intruders,—traffickers abhorr'd,
That grieve Thy loving Spirit's gentle mind,
Making the holy place, where Thou shouldst reign
Alone, a den of earthliness again.

" Thou wilt destroy this temple, for within
A fretting leprosy is on the walls.
Nor can this plague-spot of indwelling sin
Be purified until the fabric falls ;
And though, at times, to feel Thy work begin,
Dismays the shrinking flesh, yet faith recalls
The blessed hope, that as Thy word is true,
Thou wilt return and build it up anew.

" Yes, Lord ! a body glorious as Thine own
Shall upward from the dusty ruin spring ;
And the unsightly grain, in weakness sown,
Shall rise in power, a holy, heavenly thing ;
When Thou shalt come to sit on David's throne,
And rule in righteousness as Zion's King,
With all Thy risen saints.   Oh ! soon again,
Lord Jesus, come ! take Thy great power and reign !"

CHASTISEMENT is the badge of sonship. "What son is he whom the father chasteneth not?" In the "household of God" it invariably forms a part of the family discipline. "If ye be *without* chastisement, whereof all are partakers, then are ye bastards and not sons." The "Captain of our salvation" was Himself "made perfect through suffering." Not, however, suffering under the form of chastisement, which always supposes sin; for, "holy, harmless, undefiled, and separate from sinners," our spotless Emmanuel was ever the "be-loved Son," in whom the Father was "well pleased." His sufferings were endured solely for the sake of His Church, "that He might be a merciful and faithful High Priest," one who being in all points tempted like as we are, "might be touched with the feeling of our infirmities," might fully enter into the temptations, the wants, the afflic-tions of His people.

It is the suffering believer's most blessed consolation to feel assured, that every sorrow which he endures has had its counterpart in the history of Jesus. How does the firm persuasion of this precious truth soothe the bed of lan-guishing, bind up the broken heart, and sweeten every cup of bitterness — to feel, " I am not alone, my Lord is with me, He sympathises with every pang, He enters into every anxiety, He shares every burden, He knows all that I suffer, for He experienced all Himself, and He has borne pain and sorrow in His own Person, in order that He may feel for me His weak and suffering child." In none of His offices is Christ dearer to the believer than as the sharer of His every sorrow. In this capacity His perfect manhood, His ability to enter fully into every sinless infirmity, every variety of suffering, renders Him in very truth the " brother born for adversity." There *are* trials which we can tell to none but Jesus, which we could not confide even to the dearest of earthly friends. " The heart knoweth its *own* bitterness." That which is a bitter trial to me may be no trial at all to my friend, he may even be

G

disposed to smile at my weakness in considering it a trial; but it is not so with our *heavenly* Friend. "He hath not despised nor abhorred the affliction of the afflicted." Whatever weighs down the spirit, whatever saddens the heart, gives us a fresh claim upon the loving sympathy of our Saviour.

> "Whate'er the wounded spirit grieves,
> No light distress will Jesus deem;
> There's not a sigh my bosom heaves
> But stirs a kindred pulse in Him."

"O blessed Redeemer! how precious is Thy love; even 'as ointment poured forth,' healing every wound, and soothing every sorrow. Teach Thine afflicted ones so to realise Thy sympathy, so to rest in Thy love, that the consolation may outweigh the trial, and joy eclipse the grief."

In close connexion with the human sympathy of Christ, *another* blessed truth presents itself. The Lord never afflicts His people *willingly*. If it be painful to the heart of an earthly parent to inflict suffering upon a beloved child, how much more reluctant is our heavenly Father to smite the children of His adoption and love! There must be a *need* of the trial, or it would not be inflicted. Every true believer knows some little of the deceitfulness of his own heart, though his knowledge is but partial and imperfect. He has never probed the depth of his own sinfulness, he has never scanned the dark recesses of his corruptions. How much secret and deadly evil may be lurking in his soul, of which he is totally ignorant. But the Lord beholds the *full* extent of sin, for to Him " all things are naked and opened;" and although as regards His children, their " transgression is forgiven and their sin covered," the original and corrupt nature inherited from Adam still remains within them, impure and unholy as ever, and only to be crucified and kept in subjection, through the indwelling power of the Spirit. To *make manifest* and *subdue* this evil principle, is the great aim and end of God's chastenings. It is against the *sin* within them that all His efforts are directed. His "will is their sanctification," their entire conformity to the image of His beloved Son, and the Holy Spirit constrains them to desire and pray *themselves* for likemindedness to Jesus. And the Lord fulfils their desires and answers their petitions, but not always in the manner expected. In His unerring love and wisdom, our heavenly Father may see that nothing but affliction (sometimes heavy and protracted affliction) will subdue the evil propensities of the flesh, and cause the blessed fruits of the Spirit to grow and flourish in the soul. For this purpose does the Lord chasten the children of His kingdom, not in *wrath* but in *love*, not in *judgment* but in *mercy*.

"We are chastened of the Lord, that we should not be condemned with the world." It frequently happens, that while a believer is smarting under trial, he can realise nothing but his own suffering, and loses sight of the wise and loving hand which directs the stroke. He thinks it hard that he should be singled out, as it were, as "a mark for the

Lord's arrows," and "bitterness of spirit" aggravates and increases his affliction. Such was the feeling of David, when he said, " Behold, these are the ungodly, who prosper in the world ; they increase in riches. Verily I have cleansed my heart in vain, and washed my hands in innocency. For all the day long have I been plagued, and chastened every morning."

Realising nothing but his own suffering, he could not discern the Lord's love to himself, and thus envy at the prosperity of the wicked, and a murmuring and discontented spirit, took possession of his heart. But God will not suffer His children to remain under a mistaken notion of His dealings towards them. Sooner or later He will enable them both to feel and acknowledge the depth and wisdom of that love which has seen fit to afflict them for a season. " In the sanctuary of God" David learned the secret purpose of Jehovah in His afflictive dealings, and at the same time his own folly and impatience. In the light of the sanctuary, in calm undisturbed intercourse with the Saviour, all things appear under a different aspect. *Then*, in recalling our own waywardness and rebellion, we can say with David, " So foolish was I and ignorant, I was as a beast before Thee." *Then*, in retracing the gracious guidance of our heavenly Father, the unwearied pains that He bestows upon us, the depth of His love, the tenderness of His compassion, our hearts are melted beneath His loving-kindness; and again, taking up the language of the Psalmist, we ex-

claim, "Thou shalt guide me with Thy
counsel, and afterward receive me to
glory. Whom have I in heaven but
Thee? and there is none upon earth that
I desire beside Thee. My flesh and my
heart faileth, but God is the strength of
my heart, and my portion for ever."

" It is Thy hand, my God,
   My sorrow comes from Thee ;
I bow beneath Thy chastening rod,
   'Tis love that bruises me.

" I would not murmur, Lord,
   Before Thee I am dumb ;
Lest I should breathe one murmuring word,
   To Thee for help I come.

" I know Thy will is right
   Though it may seem severe,
Thy path is still unsullied light,
   Though dark it oft appear.

" Jesus for me hath died,
   Thy Son Thou didst not spare ;
His pierced hands, His bleeding side,
   Thy love for me declare.

" My God ! Thy name is love,
    A Father's hand is Thine ;
With tearful eyes I look above,
    And cry ' Thy will be mine.'

" Here my poor heart can rest,
    My God it cleaves to Thee ;
Thy will is love, Thy end is blest,
    All work for good to me."

CHAPTER IX.

Assurance.

"God so loved the world that he gave his only-begotten Son, that whosoever believeth in him should not perish, but have everlasting life."—JOHN iii. 16.

"And we have known and believed the love that God hath to us."—1 JOHN iv. 16.

"My sheep hear my voice, and I know them, and they follow me : and I give unto them eternal life ; and they shall never perish, neither shall any pluck them out of my hand. My Father, which gave them me, is greater than all ; and none is able to pluck them out of my Father's hand."—JOHN x. 27-29.

"For by one offering he hath perfected for ever them that are sanctified."—HEB. x. 14.

"Wherein God, willing more abundantly to shew unto the heirs of promise the immutability of his counsel, confirmed it by an oath : that by two immutable things, in which it was impossible for God to lie, we might have a strong consolation, who have fled for refuge to lay hold upon the hope set before us : which hope we have as an anchor of the soul, both sure and stedfast, and which entereth into that within the vail ; whither the forerunner is for us entered, even Jesus, made an high priest for ever after the order of Melchisedec."—HEB. vi. 17-20.

"For I know whom I have believed, and am persuaded that he is able to keep that which I have committed unto him against that day."—2 TIM. i. 12.

" Now I have found the blessed ground
    Where my soul's anchor may remain—
The Lamb of God, who for my sin
    Was from the world's foundation slain ;
Whose mercy shall unshaken stay
When heaven and earth are fled away.

" O Love ! thou bottomless abyss,
    My sins are swallow'd up in thee ;
Cover'd is my unrighteousness,
    From condemnation now I'm free ;
While Jesu's blood, through earth and skies,
Mercy, free, boundless mercy, cries.

" By faith I plunge me in this sea ;
    Here is my hope, my joy, my rest ;
Hither, when hell assails, I flee,
    And look into my Saviour's breast.
Away, sad doubt and anxious care !
Mercy is only written there.

" Though waves and storms go o'er my head,
    Though health, and strength, and friends be gone,
Though joys be wither'd all and fled,
    Though every comfort be withdrawn,
Steadfast on this my soul relies—
Father, Thy mercy never dies.

" Fix'd on this ground will I remain,
    Though my heart fail, and flesh decay ;
This anchor shall my soul sustain
    When earth's foundations pass away.
Mercy's full power I then shall prove,
Loved with an everlasting love."

T is a painful thought that many of the Lord's own children, who by faith "*have* fled for refuge to lay hold on the hope set before them," whose "names *are* written in the book of life," who *are* "members of Christ, and inheritors of the kingdom of heaven," are still sighing in uncertainty as to their eternal salvation. They cannot say, with the unswerving confidence of the apostle, "I *know* whom I have believed, and am *persuaded* that He is able to *keep* that which I have committed unto Him against that day." Fear, instead of hope, predominates in their hearts, and the faint hope they possess is hardly worth the name; though, such as it is, it prevents their sinking altogether into despair. But it is not like the hope which is "an anchor of the soul, both sure and steadfast, and which entereth into that within the vail;" it is not like the hope which "maketh not ashamed;" it is not like the "abounding hope" which shuts out all doubt and uncertainty, and enables the believer to say with humble confidence, "I am persuaded that neither death, nor life, nor angels, nor principalities, nor powers, nor things present, nor things to come, nor height, nor depth, nor any other creature, shall be able to separate me from the love of God, which is in Christ Jesus my Lord."

And why this painful, unsatisfactory state of mind? Why should those who have the seal of the Holy Spirit, whose hope (weak and trembling though it be) is only in the Lord Jesus,—why should they be thus "subject to bondage," thus tortured with fear and harassed with doubt?—in short,

> " Why should the children of a King
> Go mourning all their days?"

Is it the will of their heavenly Father to keep *some* of His children in a state of perpetual disquietude, of unceasing fluctuations between hope and fear, while others are enabled to say with gladness and confidence, "We have *known* and *believed* the love that God hath to us?" Oh no! It is not the *will* or (and we speak with humble reverence) the *intention* of God, that one of those who believe in His Son should perish, or even remain in uncertainty as regards their salvation. There is not a passage in the Word of God, which, rightly considered, can lead to such a conclusion. On the contrary, from the whole tenor of Scripture, it is unquestionably the will of our heavenly Father that all who believe in His Son shall have "everlasting life;" and not only have it, but *rejoice* in the possession, feeling assured that it is theirs for ever by an eternal and immutable covenant. Did St Paul for one moment question his eternal safety, when he declared with such unhesitating confidence, "I know in whom I have believed, and am persuaded that He is able to keep that which I have committed unto Him against that day?"

Or does St John doubt his acceptance when he writes, "We have known and believed the love that God hath to us?" And let it be remembered that, in themselves, neither of the apostles had any more *right* to the "full assurance of hope" than the weakest believer now sighing in fear and despondency. No, it was through faith alone—faith in the merits and blood of Jesus—that their joy and confidence survived and flourished amidst trials, and temptations, and hindrances even greater than those which beset the saints of the present day. And where lay the secret of that settled and abiding assurance, which neither men nor devils were able to destroy? We believe it was their calm and steady reliance on the love of Jesus which thus enabled them to "hold fast the beginning of their confidence steadfast unto the end." They did not dwell upon their own love to Christ, but upon His unchanging love to *them.* And while thus "looking unto Jesus," they *could* not be "moved away from the hope of the gospel;" for as the needle when it reaches the pole at once ceases to tremble, so the believer when *abiding* in Jesus is at perfect rest. "Thou wilt keep him in perfect peace whose mind is stayed on thee, because he trusteth in thee." Alas! how many saints are dwelling upon their own feeble, fluctuating love to the Saviour, and making *that* the standard of their hopes and fears! Looking into their own sinful, ever-changing hearts, for evidences of salvation, instead of reading their eternal pardon in the blood of the Redeemer, instead of resting their souls upon those precious promises which are "yea and amen in Christ Jesus." No wonder that they are like "a wave of the sea, driven with the wind and tossed." No abiding peace, no enduring hope. In *ourselves* we have everything to discourage and depress, in Christ we have everything to confirm and establish our souls. We look at our own wanderings, sinfulness, shortcomings, unfaithfulness ; and, like Peter when walking on the water, we begin at once to sink. And let us not forget that it is the constant aim of our spiritual enemy to take advantage of this tendency in the people of God, and to make it the means of hiding from their view the unchanging, ever-enduring love of Jesus. "How *can* you," he suggests to the desponding believer, "be a true child of God, with so sinful, so faithless a heart? Think of its coldness, its deadness, its aversion to spiritual exercises, its tendency to everything that is earthly. How is it possible that with such a heart as this you can really have passed from death unto life? Is not your hope a delusion? Have you not been deceiving yourself? Can genuine believers experience the same conflict with sin which is constantly passing in your own soul?" How many saints will be ready to exclaim, "This is just the picture of what passes in my own heart! Just so am I tempted and harassed, until I am ready to lose all hope, and to fear that for me there is no peace, no salvation." Ah, dear fellow-pilgrim, just so will it be as long as you look at yourself instead of looking to Jesus. You will have no enduring peace, no abiding joy. Your hope will be ever languishing, your fears ever predominating. But look upon the face of the Beloved, and behold only mercy and love. Listen to His promises, addressed to you as entirely and individually as though yours were the only case needing comfort and encouragement. "I have loved thee with an everlasting love; therefore with lovingkindness have I drawn thee." "My sheep shall never perish, neither shall any man pluck them out of my hand." "It is not the will of your Father which is in heaven that one of these little ones should perish." "Fear not, little flock, for it is your Father's good pleasure to give you the kingdom."

And here arises an oft-repeated question. "How may I know," asks an anxious soul, "that I *am* one of the sheep, one of the little flock to whom these promises are addressed?" Do you feel, dear friend, that you are a sinner? I do not ask, have you been overwhelmed with despair on account of your sins, or passed through a season of darkness and gloom—a night in which "neither sun nor stars in many days appeared?" *Some* souls are made to pass through this "valley of the shadow of death," but *all* do not. God has various ways of bringing sinners to Himself. He deals with some as with Lydia, "whose heart the Lord opened." We do not read that she experienced any fearful convictions, or passed through any season of overwhelming despair;

but we rather conclude, from the Scripture narrative, that the Lord gently drew her to Himself with the "cords of love." In the same chapter, however, we are told of a sinner who, through the terrors of a fearful earthquake, was aroused to a sense of the still deeper terrors caused by a view of his own sinfulness, and whose awakened conscience could only give vent to her alarm and despair, in the agonised cry, "What must I do to be saved?" From these narratives, placed side by side in the Word of God, the Holy Spirit would teach us that God in His sovereign wisdom often chooses very opposite means in the awakening and conversion of sinners, and, therefore, the question is, not whether you have experienced the terrors of the Philippian jailor, but whether you have, through the teaching of the Holy Spirit, been made to *know* and *feel* your own sinfulness, and, at the same time, your entire inability to save yourself.

Do you, by the teaching of the same Spirit, *know* and *realise* that your only refuge, your only hope, is in the Lord Jesus? Do you feel sin to be your greatest burden, and is it your earnest desire to be freed from its dominion? Is the feeble hope which you possess more precious to you than life itself? And, in spite of the coldness and sinfulness which you feel within, is it your earnest desire to increase in the knowledge and love of Christ? If in the sight of God your heart responds to these questions, and your conscience can add its solemn and faithful affirmative,

you are indeed one of that blessed company who can claim as their own those
"exceeding great and precious promises,
by which we are made partakers of the
Divine nature." You are one of the
" little flock to whom it is the Father's
good pleasure to give the kingdom."
You are one whom nothing can separate
from the love of Christ. You are already "risen in Him." He is ever inter-
ceding for you, ever bearing you on His
heart before God, ever guiding and sustaining you with His unseen but omnipotent hand. You are so dear to Him,
that

> " He *can't* come in glory
> And leave you behind."

"O thou of little faith, *wherefore* dost
thou doubt?" Is not your salvation
eternally secure? Is there any flaw in

the lease which makes over to you an
everlasting inheritance?—any omission
in the covenant which renders you the
purchased one of Jesus? "God, willing
more abundantly to shew unto the heirs
of promise the immutability of his
counsel, confirmed it by an oath : that
by two immutable things, in which it
was impossible for God to lie, we might
have a strong consolation, who have fled
for refuge to lay hold upon the hope set
before us."

> " A debtor to mercy alone,
>   Of covenant mercy I sing,
> Nor fear, with Thy righteousness on,
>   My person and offerings to bring.
> The terrors of law and of God
>   With me can have nothing to do ;
> A Saviour's obedience and blood
>   Hide all my transgressions from view.

> " The work which His goodness began,
>   The arm of His strength will complete ;

His promise is yea and amen,
   And never was forfeited yet.
Things future, nor things that are now,
   Nor all things below nor above,
Can make Him His promise forego,
   Or sever my soul from His love.

"My name from the palms of his hands
   Eternity will not erase;
Impress'd on his heart it remains
   In marks of indelible grace;
And I to the end shall endure,
   As sure as the earnest is given,
More happy, but not more secure,
   The glorified spirits in heaven."

Toplady.

CHAPTER X.

A Holy Walk.

" For thou hast delivered my soul from death : wilt not thou deliver my feet from falling, that I may walk before God in the light of the living."—PSALM lvi. 13.

" He that walketh righteously, and speaketh uprightly ; he that despiseth the gain of oppressions, that shaketh his hands from holding of bribes, that stoppeth his ears from hearing of blood, and shutteth his eyes from seeing evil ; he shall dwell on high : his place of defence shall be in the munitions of rocks : bread shall be given him ; his waters shall be sure. Thine eyes shall see the king in his beauty : they shall behold the land that is very far off."—ISA. xxxiii. 15–17.

" Jesus riseth from supper, and laid aside his garments ; and took a towel, and girded himself. After that he poureth water into a bason, and began to wash the disciples' feet, and to wipe them with the towel wherewith he was girded. Then cometh he to Simon Peter : and Peter saith unto him, Lord, dost thou wash my feet ? Jesus answered and said unto him, What I do thou knowest not now ; but thou shalt know hereafter. Peter saith unto him, Thou shalt never wash my feet. Jesus answered him, If I wash thee not, thou hast no part with me. Simon Peter saith unto him, Lord, not my feet only, but also my hands and my head. Jesus saith to him, He that is washed needeth not save to wash his feet, but is clean every whit."—JOHN xiii. 4–10.

" And beside this, giving all diligence, add to your faith virtue ; and to virtue knowledge ; and to knowledge temperance ; and to temperance patience ; and to patience godliness ; and to godliness brotherly kindness ; and to brotherly kindness charity. For if these things be in you, and abound, they make you that ye shall neither be barren nor unfruitful in the knowledge of our Lord Jesus Christ. But he that lacketh these things is blind, and cannot see afar off, and hath forgotten that he was purged from his old sins. Wherefore the rather, brethren, give diligence to make your calling and election sure : for if you do these things, ye shall never fall : for so an entrance shall be ministered unto you abundantly into the everlasting kingdom of our Lord and Saviour Jesus Christ."—2 PET. i. 5–11.

" Oh for a closer walk with God,
 A calm and heavenly frame,
 A light to shine upon the road
 That leads me to the Lamb !

" The dearest idol I have known,
 Whate'er that idol be,
 Help me to tear it from Thy throne,
 And worship only Thee "

COWPER.

THAT the believer's joy and peace depend upon his growing conformity to the image of his Master, upon his proximity to the treasury from whence he obtains all his spiritual supplies, is a truth distinctly and repeatedly set forth in the Word of God. Clear views of acceptance, happy fellowship with Jesus, and the enjoyment of the peace which nothing can destroy, are inseparably connected with a holy walk. " Thou *hast* delivered my soul from death," exclaims David; " wilt not thou deliver my

feet from falling, that I may walk before God in the light of the living?"
When a sinner by faith is brought near
to God, when he is pardoned, justified,
and "accepted in the beloved," he is at
once introduced into another state of
existence. "Old things are passed
away, behold, all things are become
new." He has a new course to run, and
new duties to fulfil. New desires are
awakened within him, he becomes the
possessor of new privileges, he has new
hopes, new motives of action; in short,
he is what Scripture emphatically calls
him—"*a new creature.*" His deliverance
from eternal death has been a *full, perfect*, and *complete* deliverance, and the
life which he has received is secure and
everlasting as the life of Jesus; for it is
the *same* life, the same mighty pulsation

vibrating from the risen Head, through every member of His mystical body. The feeblest believer, equally with the strongest, is a partaker of this life, which is the free gift of God, given "without money and without price."

But here arises a solemn consideration. Are believers, having received this life, to rest satisfied? Are deliverance from eternal death and the possession of everlasting life the sole objects of salvation? Let Scripture itself supply the answer. "Ye are not your own, ye are bought with a price, therefore glorify God in your body and in your spirit, which are God's." There is not through the whole Word of God a more momentous and heart-searching declaration. It enfolds the believer's eternal destiny. "Ye are not your own." No

I

longer the willing slaves of self and
Satan ; no longer the "servants of iniquity," no longer at liberty to follow the
course of this world. "Ye are bought
with a price," and that price the blood
of Christ, the blood that washed away
our sins, that sealed our pardon, that
redeemed us from death. "Therefore
glorify God in your body and in your
spirit, which are God's." Here is the
grand object of salvation—the glory of
God! For *this* we were delivered from
death, for *this* we were made partakers
of eternal life. It is that we may follow
our Redeemer, that we may tread the
path hallowed by His footsteps, that we
may live and breathe only for our
Lord's glory. The standard which is
set before us is no other than the Lord
Jesus Christ. In Him we have a perfect

model of sinless humanity. Not only did He come into the world to deliver us from eternal death, but to "leave us an example that we should follow His steps." It is impossible for the child of God to *enjoy* the full and blessed privileges of his risen life, unless his walk upon earth bear *some* resemblance to that of his Divine Exemplar. When "accepted in the Beloved," we become "children of light." "The Sun of righteousness" has arisen upon us, and the darkness of unpardoned sin has passed away. But as in the natural sky dense clouds and murky vapours may obscure the rays of the great luminary; so in the Christian soul will a careless walk produce spiritual gloom, hiding the face of Jesus, and dimming the prospect of eternal joy.

We constantly, in the Word of God, find injunctions to a holy and blameless life coupled with the most blessed promises of spiritual peace and joy. In Isa. xxxiii. 15, we have a graphic delineation of the walk of a faithful child of God. Then follows a promise: "He shall dwell on high: his place of defence shall be the munitions of rocks: bread shall be given him ; his waters shall be sure. Thine eyes shall see the king in his beauty ; they shall behold the land that is very far off." The latter verse we believe to be, not only a promise for the life to come, but of that which now is,—that even here the believer who walks in holy fellowship with his Saviour, having his heart and affections set upon things above, who habitually mortifies his corrupt inclinations, and the upright-

ness of whose walk bears testimony to
the *reality* of his profession;—we believe
that such a saint, like Moses from Pis-
gah's mount, shall by faith "behold the
land that is very far off," and, while yet
in the body, shall enjoy a foretaste of
eternal bliss. The presence of Jesus is
the believer's heaven; and "Christ in
him the hope of glory" will cause even
"the desert to rejoice and blossom as
the rose." Thus dwelling in communion
with his Lord, and enjoying the full assurance of His unchanging love, the believer journeys along with happiness
and security, singing as he goes,—

> " My heart within me leapeth,
>   And *cannot* down be cast ;
> In sunshine bright it keepeth
>   A never-ending feast.

> " The light which shines around me
>   Is Jesus Christ alone,

And what to sing invites me
Is heaven on earth begun."

How many saints in the present day
are dwarfish and sickly in soul, without
health, without vigour in their spiritual
life! And why? Because, although
they *have* received the gift of God, even
eternal life, they do not "give diligence
to make their calling and election sure."
They do not seek to maintain unbroken
fellowship with Jesus, feeding upon Him
by faith, dwelling upon His love, abiding in His embrace, "*delighting* themselves in the Lord." Their visits to the
blood of sprinkling are few and far between ; hence the burdened conscience,
the spotted garment, the dim, indistinct
views of Jesus, the dense clouds which
arise between their souls and Christ, instead of the "joy and peace in believ-

ing," the "conscience void of offence," "the garments unspotted from the world," the constant abiding in the calm sunshine of eternal love, which are the unfailing results of a holy walk, of that *practical* union with Christ, which manifests the believer's oneness with his risen Lord.

> " Walk in the light, and thou shalt own
>   Thy darkness pass'd away,
>   Because on thee the light hath shone
>   In which is perfect day.
>
> " Walk in the light, and sin abhorr'd
>   Shall not defile again ;
>   The blood of Jesus Christ the Lord
>   Shall cleanse from every stain.
>
> " Walk in the light, so shalt thou know
>   That fellowship of love,
>   His Spirit only can bestow
>   Who reigns in light above.
>
> " Walk in the light, and follow on,
>   Till faith be turn'd to sight,

When, in divine communion,
  God is Himself the light.

"Forth in Thy name, O Lord, I go,
  My daily labour to pursue;
Thee, only Thee, resolved to know,
  In all I think, or speak, or do.

"The task Thy wisdom hath assign'd,
  Oh, let me cheerfully fulfil;
In all my works Thy presence find,
  And prove Thy good and holy will.

"Give me to bear Thy easy yoke,
  And every moment watch and pray;
And still to things eternal look,
  And hasten to Thy glorious day.

"Fain would I still for Thee employ
  Whate'er Thy bounteous grace hath given,
And run my course with even joy,
  And closely walk with Thee to heaven."

CHAPTER XI.

"Meet for the Master's Use."

"Take away the dross from the silver, and there shall come forth a vessel for the finer."—Prov. xxv. 4.

"If a man therefore purge himself from these, he shall be a vessel unto honour, sanctified, and meet for the master's use, and prepared unto every good work."—2 Tim. ii. 21.

"For we are his workmanship, created in Christ Jesus unto good works, which God hath before ordained that we should walk in them."—Eph. ii. 10.

"And they shall hang upon him all the glory of his father's house, the offspring and the issue, all vessels of small quantity, from the vessels of cups, even to all the vessels of flagons."—Isa. xxii. 24.

"Not that we are sufficient of ourselves to think anything as of ourselves, but our sufficiency is of God."—2 Cor. iii. 5.

"Now the God of peace, that brought again from the dead our Lord Jesus, that great Shepherd of the sheep, through the blood of the everlasting covenant, make you perfect in every good work to do his will, working in you that which is well pleasing in his sight, through Jesus Christ; to whom be glory for ever and ever. Amen."—Heb. xiii. 20, 21.

" Father, I know that all my life
    Is portion'd out for me,
And the changes that are sure to come
    I do not fear to see ;
But I ask Thee for a patient mind,
    Intent on pleasing Thee.

" I ask Thee for a thoughtful love,
    Through constant watching wise,
To meet the glad with joyful smiles,
    And wipe the weeping eyes ;
And a heart at leisure from itself,
    To soothe and sympathise.

" I would not have the restless will
    That hurries to and fro,
Seeking for some great thing to do,
    Or secret thing to know :
I would be treated as a child,
    And guided where I go.

" Wherever in the world I am,
    In whatsoe'er estate,
I have a fellowship with hearts
    To keep and cultivate,
And a work of lowly love to do
    For the Lord on whom I wait.

" So I ask Thee for the daily strength,—
    To none that ask denied,—
And a mind to blend with outward life
    While dwelling at Thy side,
Content to fill a little space,
    If Thou be glorified.

" And if some things I do not ask
    In my cup of blessing be,
I would have my spirit fill'd the more
    With grateful love to Thee ;
And careful, less to serve Thee *much*
    Than to please Thee *perfectly*.

" There are briers besetting every path,
    That call for patient care ,
There is a cross in every lot,
    And an earnest need for prayer :
But the lowly heart that leans on Thee
    Is happy anywhere.

" In a service that Thy love appoints
    There are no bonds for me ;
For my secret heart is taught " the truth "
    That makes Thy children " free,"
And a life of self-renouncing love
    Is a life of liberty."
                                 A. L. W.

THE desire to become a labourer in his Lord's vineyard is a distinguishing feature of the sincere believer. With David, he says, "What shall I render unto the Lord for all his benefits?" He delights to take a part in the blessed work of leading souls to Christ; and while rejoicing in his own salvation, his heart yearns over those who are perishing in unbelief. He looks around him, and beholds multitudes on every side "dead in trespasses and sins," "having no hope, and without God in the world." He hears of "the dark places of the earth, which are full of the habitations of cruelty,"—of "the tears of such as are oppressed, who have no comforter,"— and he feels that the only remedy for their woes, the only balm for their wounds, is the life-giving, peace-breathing religion of Jesus.

That it is the will of God for His people to co-operate with Him in the extension of His kingdom, Scripture supplies abundant evidence. "Seek ye first the kingdom of God and his righteousness, and all these things shall be added unto you." We believe that this passage, though frequently applied to the unconverted, as an appeal urging them to seek and secure eternal life, will bear a far wider interpretation. It invites *all* who have already passed from death unto life to devote their

energies, their time, their thoughts, to
the enlargement of God's kingdom. To
give it the *first* place in their affections
and interest; to long more ardently, to
labour more earnestly, for the salvation
of souls, than for any of the riches or
honours of the present world;—such is
the will of God concerning His children.
He will have them enter (and we speak
with humble reverence) into His eternal
purposes of mercy to man's fallen race,
and seek to understand, though but in
a faint degree, the depth of love which
led Him to give His only-begotten Son
for a rebel world. Having made them
one with Himself, "partakers of the
Divine nature," He will have His people
share His own joy in the return and
salvation of repenting sinners. It is
His good pleasure to make use of His

saved ones in "bringing *other* sons unto glory," and to employ the "earthen vessels" (which His own hand has fashioned and His own breath has vivified—which, though vile and worthless in their origin, are precious in the sight of their Creator and Redeemer) in His purposes of love and mercy to the yet unawakened. Oh, exalted honour! unmerited favour! to be thus united with the Lord of glory, thus singled out to declare and manifest His wondrous love; to tell other sinners "what great things the Lord hath done for *us!*" But in what consists the *secret* of holy usefulness? Where lies the power which sends the believer "on his way rejoicing," strengthening his hands, giving unction to his whole life and conversation, and, in one word, rendering

him " meet for the Master's use ? "
Listen to the language of one who from
a dying bed takes a review of his past
life,—a life eminently devoted to the
service of his heavenly Master :—

" We find in Jesus a man (I consider Him here as the Son of man) who
has no other wish than to accomplish
the mission He has received from the
Father, and who has no other plan than
to enter into the plans of the Father, so
that, with His eyes constantly fixed
upon Him, He is only occupied in
listening to His voice that He may
follow its directions, and to discern His
will in order to execute it. . . .

" Whenever there is on man's part
this perfect accordance with the will of
God, God on His part leads us in perfect light. And thus is realised an

admirable and profound expression of the Holy Spirit : 'We are created in Jesus Christ unto good works, which God hath *prepared* that we should walk in them.'

"Here good works are presented, not as a path that we have to make out for ourselves, but as a path that God has traced, and in which we have only to walk. It is God's way, not our own ; we have only to follow this path, and we shall perform every moment the will of God. The very essence of holiness is the conformity of our will with the Divine will ; it is when we have no other plan than that of God, and no other will than the will of God, that we shall have attained true holiness—holiness that will not appear outwardly only, but that will have an inward influence—a holiness like that of Jesus Christ." *

Here lies the secret of "meetness for the Master's use." It does not consist in great talent, untiring action, skill and method in execution,—not even in profound knowledge of spiritual truths. All these are useful, all may be employed in the service of God; but they are not essential elements in that pure devotion which is the mainspring of true usefulness. That will which is most in subjection to the will of God,— that heart in which self is dethroned, and where Christ is the "first object of desire,"—that mind which most closely resembles the mind of Jesus;—these constitute the "vessel meet for the Master's use," giving a holy impetus to every

* Adolphe Monod.

K

"labour of love," every act of service, every effort for the Lord's glory.

In the present day, there is great activity, and much bustling energy, in the cause of the gospel; and vast schemes and well-organised societies are in action, which have for their object the spiritual as well as the temporal good of mankind; there is also much individual effort for the well-being of others, great and praiseworthy self-denial in relieving misery, seeking and rescuing the lost, teaching the ignorant; and to all who are thus engaged we would say, "Go forward, and the Lord prosper and bless you." But, dear fellow-Christians, let us not forget the *preparative* work,—the closet intercourse with Jesus, the still hour with God, the heart-searching, self-emptying process which must ever precede success and blessing. Let us seek to know our own nothingness. Let us ever remember that "the lowest place is the highest." It is when we realise our own emptiness, when we hang upon Jesus in all the consciousness of weakness, desiring only the Lord's glory,—it is *then* that we are "vessels meet for the Master's use," that we are ready for any service, high or low, humble or exalted; then that we are willing to do or to be whatever our Master pleases. It is then that we most closely resemble Him who "came down from heaven, not to do His own will, but the will of Him that sent Him."

> " Jesus in thy memory keep,
>   Wouldst thou be God's child and friend;
> Jesus in thy heart shrined deep—
>   Still thy gaze on Jesus bend;

In thy toiling, in thy resting,
Look to Him with every breath,—
Look to Jesus' life and death.

" Look to Jesus, till, reviving,
    Faith and love thy life-springs swell,
Strength for all good things deriving
    From Him who did all things well ;
Work as He did, in thy season,
Works which shall not fade away,—
Work while it is call'd to-day."

FRANZEN.

CHAPTER XII.

Prayer.

"Hearken unto the voice of my cry, my King, and my God: for unto thee will I pray."—PSALM v. 2.

"Pray without ceasing."—1 THESS. v. 17.

"In everything by prayer and supplication with thanksgiving let your requests be made known unto God."—PHIL. iv. 6.

"Likewise the Spirit also helpeth our infirmities: for we know not what we should pray for as we ought: but the Spirit itself maketh intercession for us with groanings which cannot be uttered."—ROM. viii. 26.

"Continue in prayer, and watch in the same with thanksgiving."—COL. iv. 2.

"Again I say unto you, That if two of you shall agree on earth as touching anything that they shall ask, it shall be done for them of my Father which is in heaven."—MATT. xviii. 19.

"And whatsoever ye shall ask in my name, that will I do, that the Father may be glorified in the Son. If ye shall ask anything in my name, I will do it."—JOHN xiv. 13, 14.

"And this is the confidence that we have in him, that, if we ask anything according to his will, he heareth us: and if we know that he hear us, whatsoever we ask, we know that we have the petitions that we desired of him."—1 JOHN v. 14, 15.

"Lord, teach us to pray."—LUKE xi. 1.

"When prayer delights thee least, then learn to say,
  'Soul, now is greatest need that thou shouldst pray.
Crooked and warp'd I am, and I would fain
Straighten myself by thy right line again.
Oh, come, warm sun, and ripen my late fruits;
Pierce, genial showers, down to my parched roots.
My well is bitter; cast therein the tree,
That sweet henceforth its brackish waters be.'
Say what is prayer, when it is prayer indeed?—
The mighty utterance of a mighty need.
The man is praying who doth press with might
Out of his darkness into God's own light.
While heat the iron in the furnace won,
Withdrawn from thence, 'twas cold and hard anon.
Flowers from their stalks divided, presently
Droop, fail, and wither in the gazer's eye.
The greenest leaf, divided from its stem,
To speedy withering doth itself condemn.
The largest river, from its fountainhead
Cut off, leaves soon a parch'd and dusty bed.
All things that live from God their sustenance wait,
And sun and moon are beggars at His gate.
All skirts extended of thy mantle hold,
When angel-hands from heaven are scattering gold."

R. C. Trench.

HAT numerous difficulties, what varied temptations beset the believer when he approaches the mercy-seat! There is no spiritual exercise in which he finds himself so encompassed by infirmities, so baffled by spiritual foes, as in this medium of intercourse with his heavenly Father. And while he feels that he *must* pray, that he cannot *live* without prayer, that he cannot continue his Christian course without prayer—he feels, at the same time, that it is frequently an almost impossible thing so to banish vain and distracting thoughts as to fix his mind and

"affections on things above," and to enjoy
that sweet and holy fellowship with his
God, for which, from his inmost soul, he
longs, and which, he is fully persuaded, is
indispensable to his happiness, his growth
in grace, and the maintenance of spiritual life. Oh! how little do we enter
into the importance and privilege of
prayer! How few, how faint, are the
true breathings of the soul! upon what
frivolous pretences are we tempted to
shorten our periods of devotion, even if
we do not altogether set them aside!
What a crowd of earthly cares and
worldly schemes thicken around us on
our approach to the mercy-seat! It
acts as a signal to our great adversary
to renew and multiply his temptations:
he appears to choose it as the most
favourable opportunity for carrying into

execution his pre-arranged plots and contrivances for disturbing our peace, and distracting, even if he cannot altogether prevent, our fellowship with God. What Christian is there but has experienced such conflicts—but has thus suffered from the malice and wiles of the evil one? Yet, blessed be God! "we are not ignorant of his devices;" and his very craft, his unwearied endeavours to overcome us, should only stir us up to greater watchfulness, to deeper consciousness of our own weakness, to more childlike trust in Jesus. Through the wisdom and love of our omnipotent Guide, even the machinations of our enemy, and the sinfulness of the corrupt nature within, are overruled in blessing to our souls. We are made to feel our feebleness; we see something of our danger, and instinctively cry for help; and the voice of His child at once "enters into the ears," and reaches the heart of our paternal friend, moving His mighty arm to succour and deliver us. Oh for a faith to realise such dangers and deliverances—a faith to make things "unseen and eternal" *present realities*, instead of speculative theories,—the simple yet invincible faith which "is the substance of things hoped for, the evidence of things not seen!"

It must never be forgotten that *that* alone is *true* prayer which is the breathing of the Holy Spirit within the heart of the believer. "We know not what we should pray for as we ought; but the Spirit itself maketh intercession for us with groanings which cannot be uttered. And he that searcheth the hearts knoweth what is the mind of the Spirit, because he maketh intercession for the saints according to the will of God." One of the special offices of the Spirit is to teach us how to pray. Without His inspiration, our prayers will be dead, formal, and worthless. But "praying in the Holy Ghost," every utterance wings its way to heaven, to be presented by our Great High Priest before the eternal throne. Knowing and believing this truth, how confidently, how trustingly may we obey the Divine command, which exhorts us to "come boldly unto the throne of grace, that we may obtain mercy and find grace to help in time of need!" To come *boldly*, we must come in *faith*, feeling assured that, when dictated by the Spirit, our petitions will be "according to the will of God," and, consequently, that they will be fully and abundantly answered. It is to the prayer of *faith alone* that a blessing is promised. "All things, whatsoever ye shall ask in prayer believing, ye shall receive." "And the prayer of faith shall save the sick." "Therefore, I say unto you, what things soever ye desire, when ye pray, believe that ye receive them, and ye shall have them."

Let us, then, *expect* and *look out* for an answer to our petitions, as Elijah did, when he prayed for rain at the top of Mount Carmel. Sooner than we anticipate may the "little cloud" make its appearance, to be followed by an abundant outpouring of blessing.

We must be made to *feel* our wants and our weaknesses, in order that we may cry to God with the faith and earnestness, the importunity and perseverance, which never fail in bringing a response. When we groan beneath a sense of inbred corruption,—when we tremble before the presence of our spiritual foes,—when we sink under the pressure of earthly cares,—when we are drinking the bitter cup of sorrow,—then the cry of alarm is *forced* from the heart, "Lord, save, or I perish," and "*immediately*" the Lord's hand is stretched out, and the poor, trembling spirit finds itself in the arms of Jesus.

"Ah!" said a dying saint, "if I were to return to life, I would, with the help of God, and in distrust of myself, give much more time to prayer than I have hitherto done, reckoning much more upon the effect of that than on my own labour; which, however, it is our duty never to neglect, but which has *no strength* but in as far as it is animated by prayer."

O believer! as you value peace of mind, fellowship with Jesus, growth in grace,—as you value every spiritual blessing, "every good and perfect gift which cometh down from the Father of lights," — cherish a spirit of prayer, "cultivate new habits of prayer." Let the attitude of your soul be a habitual uplifting of the eye of faith to God, so that every doubt, every perplexity, every need, every spiritual, as well as every temporal exigency, may resolve itself into a petition. Let prayer be the atmosphere of your soul. In this consists the true spirit of the apostolic injunction, "Pray without ceasing." Be a constant visitor at the throne of grace;

you will not come away empty, when
you go resting on the promises of the
God who "knows no variableness nor
shadow of turning." "In everything
by prayer and supplication with thanksgiving let your requests be made known
unto God. And the peace of God,
which passeth all understanding, shall
keep your hearts and minds through
Christ Jesus."

" Prayer is the breath of God in man
  Returning whence it came;
 Love is the sacred fire within,
  And prayer the rising flame.

" It gives the burden'd spirit ease,
  And soothes the troubled breast;
 Yields comfort to the mourning soul,
  And to the weary rest.

" The prayers and praises of the saints,
  Like precious odours sweet,
 Ascend and spread a rich perfume
  Around the mercy-seat.

" When God inclines the heart to pray,
    He hath an ear to hear;
To Him there's music in a groan,
    And beauty in a tear.

" The humble suppliant cannot fail
    To have his wants supplied,
Since He for sinners intercedes
    Who once for sinners died."

BEDDOME.

CHAPTER XIII.

𝔒pportunities.

"Blessed are ye that sow beside all waters, that send forth thither the feet of the ox and the ass."—ISA. xxxii. 20.

"Cast thy bread upon the waters: for thou shalt find it after many days. . . . In the morning sow thy seed, and in the evening withhold not thine hand: for thou knowest not whether shall prosper, either this or that, or whether they both shall be alike good."—ECCLES. xi. 1, 6.

"As we have therefore opportunity, let us do good unto all men, especially unto them who are of the household of faith."—GAL. vi. 10.

"Redeeming *the time*, [or, *the opportunity*,] because the days are evil."—EPH. v. 16.

"I must work the works of him that sent me, while it is day: the night cometh when no man can work."—JOHN ix. 4.

"Whatsoever thy hand findeth to do, do it with thy might; for there is no work, nor device, nor knowledge, nor wisdom, in the grave, whither thou goest."—ECCLES. ix. 10.

"Not slothful in business, fervent in spirit, serving the Lord."—ROM. xii. 11.

"Blessed is that servant, whom his Lord when he cometh shall find so doing."—MATT. xxiv. 46.

L

" Sow in the morn thy seed,
    At eve hold not thy hand :
To doubt and fear give thou no heed,
    Broadcast it o'er the land.

" Beside all waters sow,
    The highway furrows stock ;
Drop it where thorns and thistles grow,
    Scatter it on the rock.

" The good, the faithful ground,
    Expect it anywhere ;
O'er hill and dale, by plots, 'tis found ;
    Go forth, then, everywhere.

" Thou knowst not which may thrive,
    The late or early sown :
Grace keeps the precious germ alive,
    When and wherever strown.

" And duly shall appear,
    In verdure, beauty, strength,
The tender blade, the stalk, the ear,
    And the full corn at length.

" Thou canst not toil in vain :
    Cold, heat, and moist, and dry,
Shall foster and mature the grain
    For garners in the sky.

" Hence, when the glorious end,
    The day of God is come,
The angel-reapers shall descend,
    And heaven cry, " Harvest home !"

Montgomery.

UR Lord's course upon earth was an unbroken course of perfect submission to His Father's will, discovering itself in a life of unceasing, untiring self-devotion : "Lo, I come to do thy will, O God." The sole motive of Christ was the glory of His Father, His sole object the salvation of sinners. *Self* is the centre of the unrenewed heart, and even when pardoned and sanctified, the believer continues to experience and mourn over the selfish tendency of his thoughts and feelings. But the Saviour had *no* self, to Him it was a dead thing, hence His

thoughts, His affections, His sympa-
thies, were ever at leisure to attend to
the sorrows and necessities of those
around Him.   No opportunity was lost,
no word left unspoken, by which good
might be effected.   He was emphatically "ready to every good work."   No
case of sorrow or of sin found Him unprepared to meet its peculiar necessities,
and the secret of His equanimity, His
devotion, His constant preparedness for
His work, was the entire absence of self-
seeking, and the complete surrender of
every thought, and feeling, and desire,
to the will of His Father.   Simplicity
and power were strikingly combined in
the character of our blessed Saviour—
the simplicity which ever accompanies
singlemindedness, the power which ever
follows unwavering confidence in God.

In the Redeemer we behold a living example of untiring activity united with that serene composure which always characterises a truly great, and at the same time a finely-regulated mind. In His life and acts there is no bustle, no display, but a calm and quiet readiness to meet every emergency, and to improve every opportunity for doing good : " He shall not cry, nor lift up, nor cause his voice to be heard in the street." As the cool, life-giving rill flows gently onward, half hidden at times by sedgy banks and arching trees, yet refreshing and restoring everything in its course, so the Great Fountain of Life pursued His noiseless way, grace flowing from His lips, and blessings tracking His footsteps. The Lord's entire freedom from self-will and self-seeking, His perfect acquiescence and delight in the will of the Father, as expressed in David's prophetic psalm, rendered Him at all times "meet for His Father's use." "Lo, I come : in the volume of the book it is written of me, I delight to do thy will, O my God : yea, thy law is within my heart." In His nature were no "weak and beggarly elements" of earthliness or ostentation to fetter and hinder His service, every motive being essentially pure, every thought, every desire in perfect unison with His Father's will. As His chosen representative upon earth, each individual believer is called upon to follow his Lord in His path of devotion and service, and in his small measure to be a light, and comfort, and blessing to all around him. It is his duty as well as his privilege to be on the watch for opportunities of doing good, to feel that, as the purchased one of Jesus, the Lord has a *right* to his service, and a claim on all that he possesses. Every genuine believer will enter into the truth of this, since it is impossible, where there exists life and light in the soul, to be blind to a truth which is so clearly and repeatedly enforced in the Word of God. "I beseech you therefore, brethren, by the mercies of God, that ye present your bodies a *living* sacrifice, holy, acceptable unto God, which is your reasonable service."

It is to be feared, however, that even among the Lord's own people are some who, from natural indolence of character and a deficiency of faith and love, are slow and backward in putting heart and hand to the Lord's work ; who appear content to go to heaven alone, instead of directing other wandering sheep into the path of safety and peace; who will not go out of their way, either to help and comfort a fellow-believer, or to warn and arouse those who are perishing in unbelief. The faith and love of such must indeed be at a low ebb, since it is impossible for these graces to be in lively exercise without a corresponding degree of earnest and sincere desire to take an active and personal share in the Lord's work. Others there are, however, whose warm and ardent temperament continually prompts them to active service. To such it would be a real trial to be unemployed in the Lord's work. They do not need prompting and urging to activity, since a love of activity and employment is a part of their very nature. Such characters are in continual need of the Holy Spirit's restraining guidance. Impulsive and restless, they are apt to undertake too much; and, like David against Goliath, to go forth with weapons which they have not proved. God will never apportion a work to any of His people for the faithful execution of which He will not bestow the needful grace and power. How much safer, how much happier, rather to *wait* for His guidance, and to seek, by communion with the Saviour, (which never fails to empty us of self, and to throw us more entirely upon the Lord's own grace,) to be *ready* for any work that the Lord may appoint for us! Let us seek to improve opportunities for doing good as they occur, as God himself presents them to us, and puts them in our way, leaving the result with Him. A word spoken under the guidance of the Holy Spirit may prove a message of salvation to some dead soul, or a " cup of cold water " to some fainting believer. We shall never know in this world the extent of the good which God effects through the agency of His people. It would not be good for us, it might puff us up, and make us " wise in our own conceits." *Our* part is to do the work which God puts into our way, feeling that we are but vessels in His hand, channels which He deigns to honour, by conveying through them His spiritual blessings to others. A constant sense of our own nothingness and insufficiency will keep us humble, and it is the " meek and lowly in heart " whom God delights to honour. Let us also bear in mind that our work is often close at hand, though we may not perceive it. We may have our own plans and contrivances for doing good, which though very excellent in themselves, may not lead to the sphere of labour which God has appointed for us. If we receive our work *only* from Him, He will give us nothing to do for which we are unprepared or unfitted. It may be very humble work, but if it is what God has appointed for us, He will accomplish His own purposes *in* it and *by* it. It is not so much the work itself as the spirit in which it is performed, that calls down a blessing from above. Our *greatest* and *highest* work is to have our wills brought into perfect subjection to the will of God. The loftiest angel has no higher aim than this, it is the end of his creation : " Bless the Lord, ye his angels that excel in strength, that do his commandments, hearkening unto the voice of his word.   Bless ye the Lord, all ye his hosts, ye ministers of his that do his pleasure." *Readiness* to every good work does not necessarily imply talent, influence, deep doctrinal knowledge ; though useful in their places, they are not essential elements in a "vessel meet for the Master's use."   The lowly waiting upon God, the heart emptied of all but Jesus, the "conscience void of offence," the single eye to God's glory, —these constitute the closest resemblance to Him in whom the Father was " well pleased."

> " 'Tis not for man to trifle ! life is brief,
>   And sin is here.
>   Our age is but the falling of a leaf,
>   A dropping tear.

We have no time to sport away the hours ;
All must be earnest in a world like ours.

" Not *many* lives, but only *one* have we,
　　　One, only one ;
How sacred should that one life be,
　　　That narrow span !
Day after day fill'd up with blessed toil,
Hour after hour still bringing in new spoil.

" O life below !—how brief, and poor, and sad !
　　　One heavy sigh.
O life above !—how long, and fair, and glad !
　　　An endless joy.
Oh to be done with daily dying here !
Oh to begin the life in yonder sphere !

" O day of time ! how dark !—O sky and earth !
　　　How dull your hue !
O day of Christ ! how bright !—O sky and earth !
　　　Made fair and new !
Come, better Eden, with thy fresher green ;
Come, brighter Salem, gladden all the scene ! "
　　　　　　　　　HORATIUS BONAR.

" Come, labour on !
Who dares stand idle on the harvest plain,
While all around him waves the golden grain ?
And to each servant does the Master say,
    'Go work to-day !'

" Come, labour on !
Claim the high calling angels cannot share,—
To young and old the gospel gladness bear ;
Redeem the time, its hours too swiftly fly.
        The night draws nigh.

" Come, labour on !
The enemy is watching, night and day,
To sow the tares, to snatch the seed away.
While slumbering saints their duty have forgot,
        He slumber'd not.

" Come, labour on !
The toil is pleasant, the reward is sure,
Blessed are those who to the end endure ;
How full their joy, how deep their rest shall be,
        O Lord, with Thee !"

Thoughtful Hours.

CHAPTER XIV.

𝔖𝔥𝔞𝔡𝔬𝔴𝔰.

"Yea, though I walk through the valley of the shadow of death, I will fear no evil: for thou art with me; thy rod and thy staff they comfort me."—Psalm xxiii. 4.

"As a shepherd seeketh out his flock in the day that he is among his sheep that are scattered; so will I seek out my sheep, and will deliver them out of all places where they have been scattered in the cloudy and dark day."—Ezek. xxxiv. 12.

"My face is foul with weeping, and on my eyelids is the shadow of death."—Job xvi. 16.

"Our heart is not turned back, neither have our steps declined from thy way; though thou hast sore broken us in the place of dragons, and covered us with the shadow of death."—Psalm xliv. 18, 19.

". . . Now for a season, if need be, ye are in heaviness through manifold temptations: that the trial of your faith, being much more precious than of gold that perisheth, though it be tried by fire, might be found unto praise and honour and glory at the appearing of Jesus Christ."—1 Pet. i. 6, 7.

"Until the day break, and the shadows flee away, I will get me to the mountain of myrrh, and to the hill of frankincense."—Cant. iv. 6.

" No shadows yonder !
   All light and song !
Each day I wonder,
   And say, How long
Shall time me sunder
   From that dear throng?

" No weeping yonder!
   All fled away !
While here I wander
   Each weary day,
And sigh as I ponder
   My long, long stay.

" No partings yonder !
   Time and space never
Again shall sunder ;
   Hearts cannot sever ;
Dearer and fonder
   Hands clasp for ever.

" None wanting yonder !
   Bought by the Lamb,
All gather'd under
   The ever-green palm.
Loud as night's thunder
   Ascends the glad psalm."

HORATIUS BONAR.

WHILE passing through this world, the believer's is a chequered life—a life of alternate lights and shadows. He has his seasons of bright sunshine, his foretastes of celestial bliss, his moments of calm and peaceful enjoyment, when by faith he "beholds the land that is very far off," and rejoices in the sunlight of his Saviour's smile, and the calm, unquestioning assurance of His changeless love. But he has also his days of darkness and gloominess, when shadows lie heavily upon his path, when his "soul is bowed down within him," when (though still retaining the "hope of salvation") the light of his Lord's countenance is hidden, and there is no happy realisation of His presence and love.

Such a state of soul is the unfailing result of a careless walk, of allowed sin, of any hidden sin, which, lurking in the heart, brings guilt upon the conscience, and hinders the free communion of the spirit with its God.

Dense and gloomy are the shadows caused by our own failures and sins; and although the wisdom and love of our heavenly Father overrules even the sinful wanderings of His children to their own‑profit, making them the means of spiritual instruction, and bringing home to their hearts not only their own weakness and folly when left to themselves, but His own gracious long-suffering and mercy ; yet should these humbling discoveries of his sinfulness and innate corruption create and foster in the child of God that lowly and self-renouncing spirit which will lead him in deep humility to cast his soul afresh upon his almighty Saviour, clinging in helpless dependence to the love which knows " no variableness, neither shadow of turning."

The darkest cloud which lowers upon the Christian's path is "the plague of his own heart." Oh, how bitter, how stinging are the trials caused by our internal foe! No wonder that the consciousness of its hateful presence within constrains the believer to cry with St Paul, "Who shall deliver me from this body of death ?" and although faith can take up the words of the same apostle and reply, " I thank God, through Jesus Christ our Lord : there is therefore now *no condemnation* to them that are in Christ Jesus;" still does the presence of that inbred corruption (from which we shall never be free until "clothed upon with our house which is from heaven") continually hinder the joy and disturb the peace of our spiritual course. There is a *bitterness* in sin, in the sorrow and darkness caused by our own failures, unlike the sweet persuasion of a Father's love in those gentle strokes which, though they penetrate the inmost soul, speak only of tenderness and grace. When bereavement takes the loved one from our side,—when the links which bind us to this world are loosened, and we feel a void in our hearts which Jesus

alone can fill,—when the " vacant chair "
and the silent grave in the churchyard
remind us that "one is not;"—at such a
time, when "the shadow of death" has
visited our dwelling, summoning one
dear as our own life to the mansions
above, how does the sweet assurance of
God's unerring love sweeten the bitter
cup, and pour wine and oil into the
wounded spirit! *Faith* can look upward and say, even with weeping eyes
and a bleeding heart, "*Himself* hath
done it;" "Even so, Father; for so it
seemed good in thy sight." This is a
cloud indeed, casting a shadow on our
onward way, never to be entirely removed until reunion restores our lost
ones; but, blessed be God, it is (when
we can confidently believe that they
have fallen asleep in Jesus) a "cloud

with a silver lining," for behind it is the "Sun of Righteousness," ready, with "healing in His wings," "to comfort all that mourn; . . . to give unto them beauty for ashes, the oil of joy for mourning, the garment of praise for the spirit of heaviness."

When sickness lays us low,—when "wearisome nights are appointed us," and the throbbing head and aching body can find no rest, how graciously does "Jesus himself draw near," and with His own loving voice speak peace and consolation to the drooping spirit, cheering the gloom of the sick-room with the sunshine of His presence, and making even the weakness of the body a means of drawing the soul nearer to Himself! And yet again, when the dark cloud of adversity breaks over the believer's head,—when "riches take to themselves wings and flee away,"—when want and penury actually present themselves to his view, and the shadowy future opens before them as a bleak and arid waste;—how confidently does his soul rest upon the "great and precious promises," whose value can only be realised in the hour of trial! It is then that the spirit feels the need of them; and not till then can the saint fully enter into their wondrous power to sustain and console the heart even in the season of deepest sorrow.

To Jesus this world was a wilderness of shadows and gloom. He could say, "*All* thy billows and thy waves are gone over me;" "Behold, all ye that pass by, and see if there be any sorrow like unto my sorrow." He drank to its

dregs the cup of woe.   And wherefore?
Not only to make atonement for us, but
that He might fully sympathise with
the afflictions of His people.   There is
no trial however bitter, no pang however
sharp, which falls to the believer's lot,
which His Redeemer has not already
experienced.   The consolation and preciousness of this truth can never be so
truly realised as in the time of need.
Then we feel its sustaining power; and
when the wildest storm arises, "fear no
evil," because our Shepherd is with us,
because "He knoweth our walking
through this great wilderness," having Himself traversed its length and
breadth as "a man of sorrows, and
acquainted with grief."   The afflictions
of this present life, the bereavements,
the privations, the bodily ailments, the

mental trials of the saint, how do they quicken his desire to gain his everlasting home! how does he strain his weary eyes in watching for the day-dawn when "the shadows shall for ever flee away," and the endless day of unclouded bliss shall banish every sorrow! How does he long for the coming of his Lord, for the glorious moment when (delivered *for ever* from the indwelling sin which is now his sorest cross, his heaviest burden) he shall rise in the image of his Saviour, pure, sinless, and immortal, to "be for ever with the Lord."

> " Brief life is *here* our portion,
>   Brief sorrow, short-lived care ;
> The life that knows no ending,
>   The tearless life, is *there.*

> " O happy tribulation !
>   Short toil, eternal rest ;
> For mortals and for sinners
>   A mansion with the blest.

" And now we fight the battle;
  But then shall wear the crown
Of full, and everlasting,
  And passionless renown.

" The morning shall awaken,
  The shadows flee away,
And each true-hearted servant
  Shall shine as doth the day.

" There God, our King and Portion,
  In fulness of His grace,
Shall we behold for ever,
  And worship face to face.

" O sweet and blessed country.
  The home of God's elect !
O sweet and blessed country
  That eager hearts expect !

" Jesus, in mercy bring us
  To that dear land of rest,—
Who art, with God the Father
  And Spirit, ever blest."
       BERNARD.

CHAPTER XV.

𝔚aiting for 𝔊od.

· ———

" The Lord is good unto them that wait for him, to the soul that seeketh him. It is good that a man should both hope and quietly wait for the salvation of the Lord."—LAM. iii. 25, 26.

"And therefore will the Lord wait, that he may be gracious unto you, and therefore will he be exalted, that he may have mercy upon you : for the Lord is a God of judgment : blessed are all they that wait for him."—ISA. xxx. 18.

" For since the beginning of the world men have not heard, nor perceived by the ear, neither hath the eye seen, O God, beside thee, what he hath prepared for him that waiteth for him."—ISA. lxiv. 4.

" I waited patiently for the Lord ; and he inclined unto me, and heard my cry."—PSALM xl. 1.

"My soul, wait thou only upon God ; for my expectation is from him."—PSALM lxii. 5.

" I wait for the Lord, my soul doth wait, and in his word do I hope. My soul waiteth for the Lord more than they that watch for the morning : I say, more than they that watch for the morning."—PSALM cxxx. 5, 6.

"Therefore I will look unto the Lord ; I will wait for the God of my salvation : my God will hear me."—MICAH vii. 7.

" They shall not be ashamed that wait for me."—ISA. xlix. 23.

" Whate'er my God ordains is right,
  His will is ever just ;
Howe'er He order now my cause
  I will be still and trust.
      He is my God—
      Though dark my road,
He holds me that I shall not fall ;
Wherefore to Him I leave it all.

" Whate'er my God ordains is right,
  He never will deceive ;
He leads me by the proper path,
  And so to Him I cleave,
      And take content
      What He hath sent ;
His hand can turn my griefs away,
And patiently I wait His day.

" Whate'er my God ordains is right,
  Here will I take my stand ;
Though sorrow, need, or death make earth
  For me a desert land.
      My Father's care
      Is round me there ;
He holds me that I shall not fall,
And so to Him I leave it all."

                    S. RODIGAST.

GREAT part of our wilderness-training consists in *waiting* for God—waiting for the unfolding of His purposes, for the guidance of His hand, for His answer to our petitions. As the Israelites *waited* for the pillar of cloud, "and when it *tarried* long upon the tabernacle," "journeyed not," so in his desert-wanderings is the believer continually called upon to "tarry* the Lord's leisure." The *cause* of the tarriance may be hidden, and impatience and self-will may fret and won-

---

* Psalm xxvii. 16, Prayer-Book version.

der at the delay, but *faith* will enable
him calmly and patiently to wait the
Lord's own time, who at the right moment, and not till then, will answer the
prayer, bestow the blessing, and clear
away the difficulty. To the *natural*
heart all this is utterly distasteful. The
children of this world, like Passion in
the "Pilgrim's Progress," "desire to
have their good things *now*," and in-
finitely prefer using their own judgment,
and depending upon their own exer-
tions, than waiting in childlike confidence upon God. They "lean upon
their own understandings," they trust to
their own efforts, and neither seek nor
desire "counsel from the Lord." They
live *practically* as if there were no God,
but as if they themselves were the sole
arbiters of their lives and destinies.

Very frequently their plans and under-
takings appear outwardly to succeed
and flourish, "for the children of this
world are in their generation wiser than
the children of light." " Behold, these
are the ungodly, who prosper in the
world, they increase in riches." Filled
with pride and self-sufficiency at the
success of their own schemes, they despise the patient endurance of the saint,
and sneer at his apparent want of energy and lack of worldly wisdom, not
knowing that a secret but unerring hand
is guiding all his affairs ; that *love, infinite love*, is watching his every step,
and ordering aright the minutest con-
cerns of his daily life. Oh ! if the vail
with which " the god of this world hath
blinded the eyes of them which believe
not " were for one moment drawn aside,

revealing the actual dangers of their perilous position, as heedless and self-confident they trifle upon the borders of hell, how would their "laughter be turned to mourning, and their joy to heaviness!" Then would the calm confidence of the saint appear in its true light, not as heedless folly or rash enthusiasm, but as a child's loving trust in a heavenly Father's wisdom, as human weakness reposing on Divine strength.

From the commencement of his spiritual course the believer is called upon to *wait* for God. He *waits* for the possession of his promised inheritance, for the fruition of those spiritual blessings which are now only in the bud. "Men have not heard, nor perceived by the ear, neither hath the eye seen, O God, beside thee, what he hath prepared for

him that waiteth for him." He *waits*
for his complete deliverance from that
corrupt nature which, even in his renewed state, still remains within him,
and often mars his peace and interrupts
his fellowship with his Lord. He waits
for the final conquest of his great adversary the devil, and for his eternal
separation from "this present evil
world;" for although, according to his
faith, he is even now partially delivered
from his spiritual enemies, his complete
emancipation will not take place until
he is "absent from the body, and present with the Lord." Even in the midst
of present darkness and uncertainty, the
true Christian ever experiences a blessed
satisfaction in "waiting patiently for the
Lord," in the full persuasion that at the
right time the darkness and suspense

N

will give way to clear, unclouded light.
The ungodly are often suffered to go on
in their own way without let or hindrance—to lay their plans, (which, as far
as this world is concerned, are often
very wise and prudent,) "to go into
such a city, and buy and sell and get
gain," to "heap up riches," and *appar-
ently* to prosper in all that they undertake. But what, alas! is the *end*, the
consummation of all their worldly prosperity and grandeur? "The wicked
passed away, and, lo, he was not; yea,
I sought him, but he could not be
found!" "The end of the wicked shall
be cut off." Far different are the Lord's
dealings with His people. He disappoints their schemes, He overturns their
projects, He withers their gourds; and
wherefore? That their love, their joy,

and their desire, may be all centred in Himself; that they may not nestle down among the good things of this world, forgetting their eternal home, forgetting their heavenly Bridegroom, forgetting that this is not their rest, and that they are but strangers here. He calls out and strengthens their faith, their patience, their submission, by making them *wait*, sometimes for long years, sometimes for their whole lives, the unfoldings of His providence, the answers to their petitions, and cuts off their expectations from other channels, disappoints their hopes from other sources, that they may "wait only upon Him."

O believer! dost thou murmur because the answer to thy prayer is long in coming? Art thou chafed and irritated because thy Father still sees a "needs be" for the season of suspense ? "*Fret not.*" The blessing will not be delayed one moment too long. "Though it tarry, *wait* for it." Seek not to bring God's purposes to pass in thine own way; such contrivances never succeed. Sarah did so, when unbelief and impatience led her to doubt the fulfilment of the Lord's promise. And, oh, what sin, what unhappiness, what confusion, did she bring upon herself and her family! And, after all, when the Lord's full time was come, the promised son was sent.

"Wait thou *only* upon God." Cease from thine own efforts, from all human appliances. "Cease ye from man, whose breath is in his nostrils ; for wherein is he to be accounted of ?" *Wait* for the development of God's purposes. He cannot be too late. He will answer thy prayer, and clear thy way at the right moment. We may tax our own strength, and use our own wisdom, but to no purpose.

> " For when our poor efforts quite fail,
> He comes in *good time* and does all."

What blessed lessons do we learn while thus *waiting* for God! We learn to "hope in His word." During the long season of suspense, how rich and precious are the promises which, one after another, give out their sweetness and fragrance for our comfort and sustenance!

How do we "grow in the knowledge of our Lord Jesus Christ!"—of His love, His compassion, His sympathy! He too is *waiting*, waiting until He shall receive His bride, until she shall be presented to Him "without spot, or wrinkle, or any such thing." *Here* she has many

spots, many blemishes ; but her wilderness-discipline is even now preparing
her for the glorious bridal day, when
she shall be for ever united to her heavenly Bridegroom.

> " Give to the winds thy fears,
>   Hope, and be undismay'd ;
> God hears thy sighs, and counts thy tears,
>   God shall lift up thy head.
>
> " Through waves, and clouds, and storms,
>   He gently clears thy way ;
> *Wait thou His time ;* so shall the night
>   Soon end in joyous day.
>
> " Still heavy is thy heart ?
>   Still sink thy spirits down ?
> Cast off the weight, let fear depart,
>   And every care be gone.
>
> " What though thou rulest not,
>   Yet heaven, and earth, and hell,
> Proclaim God sitteth on the throne,
>   And ruleth all things well.
>
> " Leave to His sovereign sway,
>   To choose and to command ;
> With wonder fill'd, thou soon shalt own
>   How wise, how strong His hand !"

CHAPTER XVI.

Reviving.

"Wilt thou not revive us again : that thy people may rejoice in thee?"—Psalm lxxxv. 6.

"Though I walk in the midst of trouble, thou wilt revive me."—Psalm cxxxviii. 7.

"O Lord, revive thy work in the midst of the years."—Hab. iii. 2.

"Restore unto me the joy of thy salvation ; and uphold me with thy free spirit."—Psalm li. 12.

"He restoreth my soul."—Psalm xxiii. 3.

"For thus saith the high and lofty One that inhabiteth eternity, whose name is Holy ; I dwell in the high and holy place, with him also that is of a contrite and humble spirit, to revive the spirit of the humble, and to revive the heart of the contrite ones."—Isa. lvii. 15.

"They that dwell under his shadow shall return ; they shall revive as the corn, and grow as the vine : the scent thereof shall be as the wine of Lebanon."—Hos. xiv. 7.

"I have seen his ways, and will heal him : I will lead him also, and restore comforts unto him and to his mourners."—Isa. vii. 18.

"They that wait upon the Lord shall renew their strength."—Isa. xl. 31.

" When darkness long has veil'd my mind,
    And smiling day once more appears,
Then, Jesus, then it is I find
    The folly of my doubts and fears.

" I chide my unbelieving heart,
    And blush that I should ever be
Thus prone to act so base a part,
    Or harbour one hard thought of Thee.

" Oh ! let me then at length be taught
    What I am still so slow to learn—
That God is love, and changes not,
    Nor knows the shadow of a turn.

" Sweet truth, and easy to repeat !
    But when my faith is sharply tried,
I find myself a learner yet,
    Unskilful, weak, and apt to slide.

" But, O my Lord ! one look from Thee
    Subdues my disobedient will,
Drives doubt and discontent away,
    And Thy rebellious worm is still.

" Thou art as ready to forgive
    As I am ready to repine ;
Thou therefore all the praise receive,
    Be shame and self-abhorrence mine."

COWPER.

EVERY sincere believer must be painfully conscious that he has within him a constant tendency to *degenerate*, to depart from God, to "forget his resting-place," to grow lukewarm, careless, and unwatchful. How often does he find himself so cold, so worldly, so averse to spiritual things, so unlike the Saviour in his thoughts, his words, his actions, that he is ready to doubt whether he can *be* a child of God, and to exclaim, "If it be so, why am I thus?" In such a state of mind, Satan is always at hand, to suggest

doubts of acceptance, despairing
thoughts, questionings of the Lord's
love and faithfulness, and too frequently
succeeds in raising what *appears to be* an
insurmountable barrier between the soul
and God.   Ever on the watch to disturb
the peace and joy of the Christian pilgrim, and far more intimately acquainted
than we are disposed to imagine with
the fluctuations and changes in our spiritual life, he is continually ready to suit
his temptations to the believer's frame
of mind, and to the peculiarities of his
character ; and although perfectly aware
that, in the case of a *true* child of God,
his power is but limited, and that he
cannot *finally* destroy the soul who has
once taken firm hold of Jesus, he still
knows that, to a certain extent, he *may*
succeed in harassing and unsettling it.

We do not sufficiently remember the immense power and cunning possessed by our great adversary, and it is his policy to *keep* us "ignorant of his devices," that thus he may "get an advantage over us." It is only by "watching unto prayer," and meeting the attacks of his malice and craft with faith and sobriety, that we shall be enabled, by God's grace, to escape his snares and machinations. "Be sober, be vigilant; *because* your adversary the devil, as a roaring lion, walketh about, seeking whom he may devour: whom resist steadfast in the faith," (1 Pet. v. 8, 9.) There is, alas! so much remaining corruption in every child of God, so much unsubdued sin, so much to *encourage* the devil in his designs and attacks, that he too frequently effects an easy entrance even into the renewed heart. Oh, how needful is it ever to bear in mind that the *old* Adam *still* remains within us, and continues just what it has always been, " deceitful above all things, and desperately wicked !" It is *incapable* of improvement, and will remain to the close of our wilderness-journey a clog and hindrance to our spiritual course, unless mortified, and kept in rigid subjection, by the indwelling power of the Holy Ghost. The flesh, in the believer, must be looked upon as a thing to be habitually *denied* and opposed ; and in proportion to this will be the healthy and vigorous state of the new and spiritual life. " Therefore, brethren, we are debtors, *not to the flesh*, to live after the flesh. For if ye live after the flesh, ye shall die ; but if ye through the Spirit do mortify the deeds of the body, ye shall live," (Rom. viii. 12, 13.)

It is the practical neglect of this solemn declaration which causes, in the experience of many saints, so many failures, so many departures from God, such decay and relapse in the spiritual life. Worldliness creeps into the heart, Christian graces droop and languish, love grows cold, faith and hope become dim; and nothing less than a *"fresh anointing"* of the Spirit, a *renewal* of Divine grace and power, a *reviving* of "the things which remain and are ready to die," can invigorate the feeble tone of the spiritual system, and restore "joy and peace in believing." For there can be no joy in the soul which through a careless walk and a worldly spirit has wandered from Jesus; there can be no peace in a heart that has been drawn aside from its true centre of repose by the attractions of inferior objects. "Wilt thou not *revive* us again, that thy people may *rejoice* in thee?" Thus prayed David when sensible of his own and his people's departure of heart from God,— when sensible of the declensions which obstructed and hindered spiritual joy. There is not an hour of the day in which the child of God (who is seeking to walk in close and happy communion with his Saviour) does not feel the need of *reviving* and *renewing* grace. The strength of *yesterday* will not suffice for the spiritual exigencies of to-day. As the manna was to be gathered day by day, so must the believer maintain a daily and hourly intercourse with the great Fountain of his spiritual supplies. He must learn by his own failures his need of continual "waiting upon the Lord," that he may "*renew* his strength,"—of "dwelling under the shadow" of Jesus, that he may "revive as the corn, and grow as the vine." Yesterday, we may have been feeding so blessedly upon the Word of God, realising so sweetly the love of Christ, and experiencing so happily the joy of believing, as to exclaim with David, "I shall *never* be moved. Lord, by thy favour thou hast made my mountain to stand strong." *To-day*, all may be changed. The Bible may be as a sealed book, Christ may seem afar off, and the soul feel cold and lifeless; and wherefore? Because (vainly endeavouring to live upon past grace) we have neglected to *renew* our strength by a fresh application to our spiritual storehouse. O believer! watch against spiritual declension; against the *beginning* of a retrograde movement. Let thy visits to the fountain be so constant that the slightest stain of guilt may at once be removed. Cherish a tender conscience, a quick perception of the presence of sin in the heart; and if conscious of the faintest change in the barometer of the soul,—of the scarcely perceptible movement which is leading thee away from peace and the Saviour, —lose no time in repairing to the only source from whence thy waning strength can be *renewed.* Seek once more the "living fountain," which at the commencement of thy pilgrimage "washed away thy sins," and there cleanse the stains with which unsubdued sin, worldlymindedness, and a careless walk, have

sullied thy garments. Let the prayer
of thy heart ascend to the mercy-seat:
" Lord, *revive* thy work in the midst of
the years, *restore* my soul, *renew* my
strength, that I may go on my way
rejoicing." Thus, *living* near the cross,
abiding in Jesus, repairing habitually to
the "fountain opened for sin and uncleanness," thou shalt be preserved from
the fearful condition of a backslider;
"thy garments shall be always white,
and thy head shall lack no ointment;"
Satan shall not obtain "an advantage
over thee;" the world and its attractions
shall lose their power; and the evil
nature within, being habitually subdued,
shall be unable to regain its ancient dominion. Thus, abiding in Christ, and
thereby growing into His image, thine
onward course shall be "as the shining

O

light, which shineth more and more unto
the perfect day."

"I do not doubt my safety—that Thy hand
  Will still uphold me, even to the last;
And that my feet on Canaan's hill shall stand,
  When the long wilderness is overpast;
But often faith is weak, and hope is low,
Forward, indeed, but faint and wearily, I go.

"I do not doubt Thy love, my Lord, my God;
  The love which suffer'd and which died for me;
The love which sought me on the downward road,
  Unclasp'd the fetters, set the captive free!
But mine seems now so languid, dull, and cold;
Oh for the blissful hours which I have known of old!

"I do not doubt, unworthy though I be,—
  Thy worthiness, my Saviour, is my own!—
One of Thy many mansions is for me,
  In the good land where sorrow is unknown;
But often clouds obscure the distant scene,
And from the flood I shrink which darkly rolls be-
    tween.

"Lord, at the evening time let there be light,
  Unveil Thy presence, bid all darkness fly;
Surely, ere now, far spent must be the night,
  The morning comes, the journey's end is nigh;
Renew my strength, what yet remains to run,
Till glory crown the work which faith has here be-
    gun."

CHAPTER XVII.

𝕿𝖍𝖊 𝖂𝖔𝖗𝖉 𝖔𝖋 𝕲𝖔𝖉.

"Being born again, not of corruptible seed, but of incorruptible, by the word of God, which liveth and abideth for ever."—1 PET. i. 23.

"The seed is the word of God."—LUKE viii. 11.

"As new-born babes, desire the sincere milk of the word, that ye may grow thereby."—1 PET. ii. 2.

"Thy words were found, and I did eat them; and thy word was unto me the joy and rejoicing of mine heart: for I am called by thy name, O Lord God of hosts."—JER. xv. 16.

"Thy word is a lamp unto my feet, and a light unto my path."—PSALM cxix. 105.

"For the commandment is a lamp; and the law is light; and reproofs of instruction are the way of life."—PROV. vi. 23.

"O how love I thy law! it is my meditation all the day."—PSALM cxix. 97.

"Whatsoever things were written aforetime were written for our learning; that we, through patience and comfort of the scriptures, might have hope."—ROM. xv. 4.

"All scripture is given by inspiration of God, and is profitable for doctrine, for reproof, for correction, for instruction in righteousness; that the man of God may be perfect, thoroughly furnished unto all good works."—2 TIM. iii 16, 17.

" Lord, Thy word abideth,
  And our footsteps guideth;
  Who its truth believeth
  Light and joy receiveth.

" When our foes are near us
  Then Thy word doth cheer us,—
  Word of consolation,
  Message of salvation.

" When the stars are o'er us,
  And dark clouds before us,
  Then its light directeth,
  And our way protecteth.

" Who can tell the pleasure,
  Who recount the treasure
  By Thy word imparted
  To the simple-hearted?

" Word of mercy, giving
  Succour to the living!
  Word of life, supplying
  Comfort to the dying!

" Oh that we, discerning
  Its most holy learning,
  Lord, may love and fear Thee,
  Evermore be near Thee!"

I T is through the teaching of the word that the sinner is first awakened to a knowledge of his danger and condemnation; and it is when this "incorruptible seed" takes root in his heart that he is "born again," and becomes a "new creature." But although the inspired Word of God contains the vitalising principle of regeneration, it is only by the power and application of the Holy Spirit that it can quicken a dead soul. The tiny seed contains the germ of life; but not until acted upon by the genial influences of sun and rain is it awakened to animation. Without the direct agency of the Holy Spirit, the Bible will be but a dead letter, neither giving life to the sinner nor sustaining and nourishing the saint. It is only when we are enabled, under His teaching, to discern Christ as the Alpha and Omega, the sum and substance of the written word, that our souls are quickened, fed, and kept alive by its vivifying truths.

"The words that I speak unto you, they are spirit and they are life."

It is very possible to be *intellectually* acquainted with the truths and doctrines of Scripture, whilst the heart remains in all its original depravity, unchanged and unblessed. It is a fundamental truth, which cannot be too deeply engrafted into the heart, that no teaching but that of the Holy Spirit can abidingly enlighten the soul.

By His power alone do the "words of Christ" come home to us as words of "spirit and life."

God, in His sovereign will, may use various *channels* in conveying His truths to the heart; "but all these worketh that one and the self-same Spirit."

Hence, it is not on the power and gifts of the *channel,* but on the *working* of the Spirit, that the blessing depends.

"Not by might nor by power, but *by my Spirit,* saith the Lord of hosts."

How prone are we to place our hopes and dependence on the creature, rather than (looking above all human means) to make *God himself* the centre of our desires and expectations! Without the Spirit, not one real prayer can ascend from our hearts to the mercy-seat; and, in like manner, without the Spirit, not one word of Divine truth can be savingly blessed to our souls. Knowing and experiencing this, what need have we (if, indeed, we are "born from above") to seek the teaching and guidance of the Holy Spirit, that whether we hear or study the written word, it may never be to us a mere dead letter, a "lovely song of one that hath a pleasant voice," but a life-giving, soul-sustaining message from our heavenly Father. Love to the Word of God is a distinguishing feature of real conversion. As a healthy infant, when ushered into existence, at once requires and cries for food, so does the new-born soul "desire the sincere milk of the word;" and in proportion to the growth and vigour of

the spiritual being will be the hunger-
ing and thirsting after this Divine nour-
ishment. Disinclination for the word is
an unfailing symptom of relapse in the
spiritual life. "Our soul *loatheth* this
light bread," exclaimed the Israelites,
when (tired of their heavenly food) they
longed for the flesh-pots of Egypt. We
may wonder at the ingratitude and discontent of the Lord's chosen people;
but, alas! can we not discern in their
failures and chastisements the facsimile
of our own spiritual history? How apt
are we to be weary of the same oft-
repeated truths, and to long for some
newer and more exciting form of ali-
ment! Oh, let us beware lest, in reject-
ing the pure and simple gospel, which
alone "is able to make us wise unto salvation," we fulfil in our own experience

the prophetic declaration of the apostle: "The time will come when they will not endure sound doctrine; but after their own lusts shall they heap to themselves teachers, having itching ears; and they shall turn away their ears from the truth, and shall be turned unto fables."

In the present day, when error is rife, and when it is continually presenting new forms of allurement (often very attractive and plausible) to entrap the heedless and unwary, what need have we of the unerring and infallible guidance of the Divine Spirit, to steer us safely through the shoals and quicksands of false doctrine, and to enlighten our understandings, that we may receive and retain nothing but the pure, unadulterated truth. To the earnest, spiritually-minded saint, who is longing for the return of his Lord, and to whom this life at best is but a weary pilgrimage, how sustaining are the truths of inspiration! "Ye have need of patience, that, after ye have done the will of God, ye might receive the promise. For yet a little while, and He that shall come will come, and will not tarry."

Although but a "little while" compared to the "for ever" of eternity,—a "light affliction" compared to the "far more exceeding and eternal weight of glory,"—the Christian traveller is often "discouraged because of the way." Sorrows press heavily upon his spirit; the weight of the flesh is at times all but insupportable; he is weary of the world, weary of his temptations, weary of himself, weary of all but Christ. At such seasons, how

blessedly does the Word of God cheer
and sustain his soul! and, leaning upon
its promises, how is his hope revived, his
patience renewed, his faith strengthened,
and his whole spiritual being refreshed
and comforted! "Whatsoever things
were written aforetime were written for
our learning, that we, through patience
and comfort of the scriptures, might
have hope." "*Patience* and *comfort!*"
How unceasingly does the believer feel
his need of them! *Patience* in waiting
for the *fulfilment* of those "great and
precious promises" upon which (in faith
and hope) his soul is now resting.
Patience during the delay of his Lord's
return. *Patience* under those daily
trials, temptations, and provocations
which have such a continual tendency
to chafe and irritate his spirit. *Comfort,*

to sustain him when laden with cares and oppressed with sorrows, when bereavement and adversity darken his home, when the hand of God "stirs up" his earthly nest, or when soul-troubles overwhelm his spirit. At such times, what language can adequately express the value and preciousness of the Lord's *own* word? It comes home to the soul with a freshness and power only to be fully experienced in the season of extremity, enabling the believer to add his grateful tribute to the testimony of David: "This is my *comfort* in my affliction; for thy word hath quickened me."

"O blessed Lord! how can we praise Thee as we ought for the precious gift of Thy holy word? Enable us to feed upon it by faith, to lean upon it in the hour of sorrow, to make it our '*staff*' in the hour of weakness, and to lay it up in our hearts as a treasure beyond all price."

"Most wondrous book ! bright candle of the Lord !
Star of eternity ! the only star
By which the bark of man could navigate
The sea of life, and gain the coast of bliss
Securely ! only star which rose on time,
And on its dark and troubled billows, still,
As generation, drifting swiftly by,
Succeeded generation, threw a ray
Of heaven's own light, and to the hills of God,
The eternal hills, pointed the sinner's eye.
This book, this holy book, on every line
Mark'd with the seal of high divinity,
On every leaf bedew'd with drops of love
Divine, and with the eternal heraldry
And signature of God Almighty stamp'd
From first to last; this ray of sacred light,
This lamp, from off the everlasting throne
Mercy took down, and in the night of time
Stood, casting on the dark her gracious bow;
And evermore beseeching men, with tears
And earnest sighs, to hear, believe, and live."

POLLOK.

CHAPTER XVIII.

Strength in Weakness.

"Have mercy upon me, O Lord ; for I am weak."—Ps. vi. 2.
"My grace is sufficient for thee : for my strength is made perfect in weakness."—2 Cor. xii. 9.
"Let the weak say, I am strong."—Joel iii. 10.
"When I am weak, then am I strong."—2 Cor. xii. 10.
"Out of weakness were made strong."—Heb. xi. 34.
"Be strong in the Lord, and in the power of his might."—Eph. vi. 10.
"Go in this thy might : . . . have not I sent thee?'—Judges vi. 14

"Half feeling our own weakness,
    We place our hands in Thine ;
Knowing but half our darkness,
    We ask for light divine.

"Then when Thy strong arm holds us,
    Our weakness most we feel,
And Thy love-light around us
    Our darkness doth reveal.

"Too oft, when faithless doubtings
    Around our spirits press,
We cry, ' Can hands so feeble
    Grasp such almightiness?'

"While thus we doubt and tremble,
    Our hold still looser grows ;
While on our darkness gazing,
    Thy radiance vainly glows.

"Oh, with Thy brightness cheer us,
    And guide us by Thy hand ;
In Thy light teach us light to see,
    In Thy strength strong to stand.

"Then though our hands be feeble,
    If they but touch Thine arm,
Thy light and power shall lead us,
    And keep us strong and calm."

" IN the history of the heroes of this world there is always a critical moment which shapes their career and insures their future glory,—it is that in which a consciousness of their own strength is suddenly imparted to them. And a moment not less decisive than this, though stamped with an impress *altogether different,* is to be found in the life of every heroic servant of God,—it is that moment in which he recognises his own absolute helplessness and nothingness ; then it is that the strength of God is communicated to him from on high." There is no sin inherent in our fallen nature (and which, when *first* awakened to a sense of our lost condition, we found a hindrance to the attainment of peace) to which the believer is not prone in his *after* Christian course. We have need constantly to remember the Divine caution, "Let him that thinketh he standeth take heed lest he fall," (1 Cor. x. 12.) With the root of evil still remaining within, there is no unwatchful moment in which its evil propensities may not break out afresh. Perhaps no sin is a greater hindrance to salvation than a propensity to place at least *some* dependence on our own strength and efforts, a reluctance to view ourselves as *wholly* helpless, wholly undeserving, and *this*, as all other sinful inclinations, continues a foe to our peace

even after we have learned through the
Holy Spirit's teaching that there is no
salvation but in an entire and unreserved
reliance on Christ. The great work of a
believer's life is to keep emptied of *self*,
that he may be filled with Christ. He
has only to examine (by the light of
the Spirit) the workings of his own
heart, to discover what a constant tendency there is to depend upon his *own*
strength, his *own* efforts, to look with
complacency upon his *own* advances in
grace. He forgets that his own strength
is utter weakness, his own efforts worse
than useless, and that every victory over
temptation, every step onward, is the
result, not of his own strength and wisdom, but of the strength and wisdom of
Him through whom the weakest saint
is "more than conqueror." Self-reliance

is a quality highly esteemed by the men of this world; they admire a character depending upon its own resources, trusting to its own efforts, bold, independent, and persevering in carrying out and accomplishing its own schemes, and all this through natural strength and energy of purpose. But self-reliance is a word which must have no place in the vocabulary of *faith*. Self-reliance is a foe to the peace of a saint, a hindrance to his growth in holiness, an enemy to his Lord's glory. It is a hard, a humbling lesson to learn our own weakness; harder, and more humbling still, to put such a lesson into practice, and daily, *hourly* to lie low before God, yet in this dwells the secret of *real* power. But, oh, how much must we frequently be made to suffer before we realise this!

how many blighted hopes, and bitter
mortifications, and disappointed schemes
must the saint endure ere he feel himself
empty, worthless, helpless before God!
But when the Master's hand has indeed
been at work, when the message has
been received in faith, when the discipline has been sanctified, and the soul,
subdued and humbled, sits like Mary at
the feet of Jesus, forgetting self, the
world, all but Christ, how perfect its
peace, how exalted its position! Such
is the state of mind which renders the
weakest believer "meet for the Master's
use." In tracing the past history of
every "earthen vessel" used by the
Lord as a means of bringing to pass
His eternal purposes, we cannot but be
struck with the fact that each had to
pass through a season of discipline and

self-humiliation ere they appeared before the world as the "sent of the Lord." And the same truth, though it is more strikingly, more forcibly brought before us in the history of such individuals, is the daily experience of every genuine saint. It is a life-work to learn our own weakness and God's strength. We began to learn them when the wonders of Calvary were disclosed to our sin-stricken souls, when, helpless and guilty, we by faith laid our iniquities upon Jesus, feeling that we had no other refuge, no other hiding-place; and the same lesson is repeated in every danger, temptation, and difficulty, when, renouncing ourselves, we rest wholly upon the omnipotence of Christ. "Strong in the Lord, and in the power of his might." In such a position the believer is invincible ; proof against every foe, for " the Lord is on his side," and " if God be for us, who can be against us ?"

"Lord, what a change within us one short hour
Spent in Thy presence will avail to make!
What burdens lighten, what temptation slake,
What parched grounds refresh as with a shower!
We kneel, and all around us seems to lower;
We rise, and all, the distant and the near,
Stands forth in sunny outline, brave and clear;
We kneel, how weak! we rise, how full of power!
Why, therefore, should we do ourselves this wrong,
Or others, that we are not always strong,
That we are ever overborne with care,
That we should ever weak or heartless be,
Anxious or troubled, when with us is prayer,
And joy, and strength, and courage are with Thee?"

R. C. TRENCH.

CHAPTER XIX.

𝕷𝖎𝖌𝖍𝖙.

"God is light, and in him is no darkness at all."—1 JOHN
i. 5.

"Then spake Jesus, . . . saying, I am the light of the
world: he that followeth me shall not walk in darkness, but
shall have the light of life."—JOHN viii. 12.

"Unto you that fear my name shall the Sun of righteousness
arise with healing in his wings."—MAL. iv. 2.

"Ye were sometimes darkness, but now are ye light in the
Lord: walk as children of light."—EPH. v. 8.

"Ye are the light of the world.

"Let your light so shine before men, that they may see
your good works, and glorify your Father which is in heaven."
—MATT. v. 14, 16.

"The path of the just is as the shining light, that shineth
more and more unto the perfect day."—PROV. iv. 18.

"And the city had no need of the sun, neither of the moon,
to shine in it; for the glory of God did lighten it, and the
Lamb is the light thereof."—REV. xxi. 23.

"Let there be light! oh, speak that word again,
    Father of mercies, to this longing heart!
Come to my soul, like sunshine after rain,
    Bidding the clouds of grief and fear depart.

"Let there be light, where shades the deepest fall
    Of long-remember'd sins, remorse, despair;
Shine upon Calvary's cross, and shew me all
    Endured for me by the great Sufferer there.

"Let there be light upon the lowly tomb,
    Where grief too deep for tears has bow'd my head;
Some rays from heaven to dissipate the gloom,
    Beneath whose shadow one loved spirit fled.

"Light on the future journey, all unknown,
    The chequer'd path of life which lies before;
Light on its close—the valley dark and lone,
    The Jordan's stormy wave and distant shore.

"Why should I walk in darkness when thy light,
    O Sun of righteousness, shines here around;
When to the land where there is no more night
    Now, by Thy grace, my pilgrim steps are bound?"

From " Thoughtful Hours," by H. L. L.

"GOD is light, and in him is no darkness at all." All "true light" emanates from God. He is its source and fountain-head. Christ Jesus is the embodiment of light, for "in him dwelleth all the fulness of the Godhead bodily," (Col. ii. 9.) The Holy Spirit conveys the light into every regenerate heart.

Satan is the prince of darkness. His kingdom is a kingdom of darkness. His children are children of darkness; and he, and all who continue in his kingdom, are condemned to "the blackness of darkness for ever!"

Light is the element of a child of God. A light never to be quenched has begun to dawn in his soul; a sun never to set has risen in his heart; and although while passing through this world the light may be dimmed, and at times even shrouded in gloom, it is but for a season. "A little while," and his "sun shall no more go down;" "for the Lord shall be his everlasting light." It is the believer's happy privilege to "walk in light," to dwell close to Jesus, who is the source of light. He is journeying through a world of darkness, he is living among souls cold and lifeless as the dry bones in Ezekiel's vision; but as in the darkness of Egypt "the land of Goshen was severed in that day" from the

doomed country around, and the fa-
voured Israelites "had light in their
dwellings," so with the Lord's chosen
ones *now.* For *them* there is light in
the midst of darkness, joy when encompassed by sorrow, peace amidst the wildest storm. Oh, how great, how glorious are the privileges of believers! How
little do we realise, how little do we enjoy the spiritual blessings that even in
this life are our portion! How prone
are we to forget the lessons we have
learned; how apt to lose sight of our
ultimate destination, as inhabitants of a
city ever resplendent with the light of
Jehovah himself! How easily do the
things of time, the trifles of this world
engage our thoughts, our hopes, our
fears, not only hiding from our view the
future blessedness which is set before

us, but disturbing the peace, which
already, by faith, is our possession and
inheritance, and obscuring that heavenly
light which "is *sown* for the righteous,"
which is their birthright, the eternal gift
of God, which Jesus died to bestow upon
them, and which the Holy Spirit is ever
seeking to preserve and strengthen in
their hearts! Oh, how faithless, how unworthy of our high calling, our exalted
destiny, to suffer (through carelessness
and worldliness) this divine light to become dim and indistinct; and how painfully does our sin bring its own punishment, as we journey along in cloudiness
and gloom, instead of nearing the goal
of our hopes, cheered by the full sunshine of eternal love! "Ye are the light
of the world. A city that is set on an
hill cannot be hid."

While in the world, Christ was the re-presentative of the Father, " God mani-fest in the flesh." Believers are (or rather *ought* to be) the representatives of Jesus. To them He has intrusted (in a measure) His name and honour. Let them consider the solemn responsi-bility of such a trust. " Ye are a chosen generation, a royal priesthood, a holy nation, a peculiar people ; that ye should *shew forth* the praises [or virtues, mar-gin] of him who hath called you out of darkness into his marvellous light."

" A city that is set on a hill cannot be hid." It is when the saint is dwelling above the din and turmoil of earth, when he is *abiding* in Jesus, when " his place of defence is the munitions of rocks," when he is separate from the world, and living apart from evil, that his light shines with that pure and steady radiance which clearly proclaims the source from whence it came. It is then that he not only glorifies his heavenly Father, and cheers and animates, by his holy walk and heavenly-mindedness, his fellow-believers, but he is a living testimony to the world of the blessed effects of "pure and undefiled religion." It is the believer's privilege to have light *within* him, and light *around* him; and although his path be involved in obscurity, "unto the upright there ariseth light in the darkness," "even the night shall be light about him." One thing alone has power to plunge him in Egyptian gloom, hiding from his view the face of Jesus, and awakening in his soul doubts and misgivings with regard to his spiritual state, and that is *allowed*

sin. If it be suffered to remain uncon-
fessed, if the conscience be burdened, if
the "blood of sprinkling" be unsought,
light and peace *must* be absent. No
cloud is so dense as that which *sin* casts
upon a believer's soul. "Then spake
Jesus again unto them, saying, I am the
light of the world : he that *followeth* me
shall not walk in darkness, but shall
have the light of life." While sin is
allowed, while pardon and peace are
unsought, the disciple has ceased (for
the time) to follow his Master, he has
forsaken the "King's highway," in which
alone there is light and safety, and is on
forbidden ground; and until he retrace
his steps, until he once more return to
his "resting - place," his sun will be
eclipsed, his sky lowering, and his soul
burdened and cast down. All the

Q

warmth, all the light of the saint are drawn from the Sun of righteousness; and while dwelling *near* the source of all his spiritual blessings, carefully tracing the footsteps of his great Exemplar, and following closely in the path which He himself has trodden, while walking by the light of His Word, and led by the guidance of His Spirit, the fulfilment of God's richest promises will be hourly experienced, and the believer's path will truly be "as the shining light, that shineth more and more unto the perfect day."

> " I heard the voice of Jesus say,
>   ' I am this dark world's light ;
> Look unto me, thy morn shall rise,
>   And all thy day be bright.'
> I look'd to Jesus, and I found
>   In Him my Star, my Sun ;
> And in that light of life I 'll walk
>   Till travelling days are done."

"Wherefore, holy brethren, partakers of the heavenly calling, consider the Apostle and High Priest of our profession, Christ Jesus."

Consider Jesus ! Dwell continually upon His love, study His character, look upon "the face of the Anointed," that His glorious image may be reflected in thine own soul ; so shall thy path on earth be a path ever tending upwards, ever cheered with the warmth and light of heaven, until, in unveiled glory, the Redeemer welcome His Bride to her eternal home, to dwell with Him for ever in "the city whose builder and maker is God."

"Sun of my soul ! Thou Saviour dear,
It is not night if Thou be near :
Oh, may no earth-born cloud arise
To hide Thee from Thy servant's eyes !

" When the soft dews of kindly sleep
My wearied eyelids gently steep,
Be my last thought, how sweet to rest
For ever on my Saviour's breast !

" Abide with me from morn till eve,
For without Thee I cannot live ;
Abide with me when night is nigh,
For without Thee I dare not die.

" Thou framer of the light and dark,
Steer through the tempest Thine own ark ;
Amid the howling wintry sea
We are in port, if we have Thee.

" Come near and bless us when we wake,
Ere through the world our way we take,
Till in the ocean of Thy love
We lose ourselves in heaven above."

CHAPTER XX.

The Haven.

"Weeping may endure for a night, but joy cometh in the morning."—PSALM xxx. 5.

"They that sow in tears shall reap in joy. He that goeth forth and weepeth, bearing precious seed, shall doubtless come again with rejoicing, bringing his sheaves with him."—PSALM cxxvi. 5, 6.

"We must through much tribulation enter into the kingdom of God."—ACTS xiv. 22.

"And if children, then heirs; heirs of God, and joint-heirs with Christ: if so be that we suffer with him, that we may be also glorified together. For I reckon, that the sufferings of this present time are not worthy to be compared with the glory which shall be revealed in us."—ROM. viii. 17, 18.

"For our light affliction, which is but for a moment, worketh for us a far more exceeding and eternal weight of glory."—2 COR. iv. 17.

"So he bringeth them unto their desired haven."—PSALM cvii. 30.

"And there shall be no night there; and they need no candle, neither light of the sun; for the Lord God giveth them light: and they shall reign for ever and ever."—REV. xxii. 5.

"Thy sun shall no more go down; neither shall thy moon withdraw itself: for the Lord shall be thine everlasting light, and the days of thy mourning shall be ended."—ISA. lx. 20.

" For thee, O dear, dear country !
      Mine eyes their vigils keep
  For very love beholding
      Thy happy name they weep.

" The mention of thy glory
      Is unction to the breast,
  And medicine in sickness,
      And love, and life, and rest.

" The Lamb is all thy splendour,
      The Crucified thy praise ;
  His laud and benediction
      Thy ransom'd people raise.

" Thou hast no shore, fair ocean !
      Thou hast no time, bright day !
  Dear fountain of refreshment
      To pilgrims far away !

" They stand, those halls of Zion,
      All jubilant with song ;
  And bright with many an angel,
      And all the martyr-throng.

" And they who with their Leader
      Have conquer'd in the fight
  For ever and for ever
      Are clad in robes of white."

                                    BERNARD.

HOPE is an essential element of man's being. From childhood to age there is a continual expectation of something, which is not yet in possession. Hope will sustain the heart under an accumulation of evils; and where it predominates, it imparts a buoyancy and elasticity of spirit which it is hardly possible to overcome. Deprive a man of hope, and you deprive him of all that cheers and animates him —all that renders life interesting and joyous.

In the spiritual life *hope* is in like

manner the animating and sustaining principle of the new nature. But it is a hope altogether independent of earthly things,—a hope which has its birth from above,—a hope which looks forward to things unseen and eternal. It is awakened in the soul when the sinner first brings his sins to the feet of Jesus, and looks to Him in faith for pardon and salvation. It is strengthened and increased as the soul grows in the knowledge and love of Christ: it is lost in sight when the haven is reached, the goal won, and the spirit fully blest; blest with the actual possession of the glories which, through years of patient waiting and wilderness-discipline, it has been looking forward to and expecting.

In the Word of God we continually find the trials of the present life, and the future bliss that awaits the believer, placed in juxtaposition: the "night of weeping," the "morning of joy;" the "light affliction which is but for a moment," the "far more exceeding and eternal weight of glory;" the weeping seed-bearer, the rejoicing harvest-man, bringing his sheaves with him; the "suffering with Christ" *here* to "reign with Him" hereafter. The child of God has his *peculiar* trials; he is not only subject, with all the human race, to the pains and sorrows of mortality, but he has his *spiritual* afflictions. He groans under a continual sense of his innate corruption, of the presence of an evil principle within, from which he knows that he shall never be entirely freed, until "this mortal shall have put on immortality." How often does he find himself overcome by this indwelling enemy, though the earnest desire of his heart is to be near, and to be like the Lord Jesus! How often does sin produce a darkness and cloudiness of soul, which hide the face of the Beloved! How often do the temptations of the evil one, "coming in like a flood," overpower for a time the nature born from above, and create a conflict of contending emotions and desires! From this warfare the saint cannot be fully delivered until "the earthly house of this tabernacle be dissolved;" and, realising this, how earnestly does he long for his *complete* emancipation! Thankful, indeed, for those sweet seasons of communion with his Saviour which, while here below, so often cheer and refresh his spirit, he still feels that he can only be *satisfied* with the perfect unending bliss of eternal union with his Lord. He longs to "go no more out," to be fully and for ever freed from sin, to be fully and for ever delivered from his great adversary the devil, and from the snares of "this present evil world." He longs to be "for ever with his Lord," to be an inhabitant of the land where they have "no need of the sun, neither of the moon to shine in it," because "the glory of God doth lighten it, and the Lamb is the light thereof."

These are the hopes which cheer his wilderness-journey, and sustain him in his spiritual conflict. "I had *fainted*, unless I had *believed*, to see the goodness of the Lord in the land of the living." The *assurance* of future blessedness im-

parts *cheerfulness* as well as endurance
to the Christian pilgrim. " The joy of
the Lord is his strength ;" and the
"songs" which enliven his sojourn in
"the house of his pilgrimage "—in other
words, his mortal body—are the ebulli-
tions of a joyous and thankful heart.
The world count him a fool, because the
things of this life have no hold upon
him. They cannot understand his actu-
ating motives, they know not the secret
spring of his joy, and therefore ridicule
his enthusiasm, and sneer at his happiness ; yet is he content to "become a
fool" for Christ's sake, since he possesses
the faith which is "the substance of
things hoped for, the evidence of things
not seen." He experiences trials, bereavements, disappointments; but he is
prepared to meet them, knowing that

"through much tribulation we must enter into the kingdom of heaven."

The words of the apostle come home to his heart with a power at once thrilling and sustaining: "Beloved, think it not strange concerning the fiery trial which is to try you, as though some strange thing happened unto you. But *rejoice*, inasmuch as ye are partakers of Christ's sufferings; that when his glory shall be revealed, ye may be glad also with exceeding joy." Thus, throughout the scene of his wilderness-journey, is the believer sustained and strengthened by the "hope set before him." Thus does his heavenly Father, through "much tribulation," bring him "unto the haven where he would be."

He knows that the training and disci-

pline of the wilderness is but preparing
him for his eternal home; that each bereavement, each disappointed hope, each
departed joy, is but loosening his hold
upon earthly things, and drawing his
heart and affections to things eternal:
and as one tie after another is sundered,
as wave after wave drives his bark
nearer to her mooring, how does he long
for the moment when his "vile body shall
be fashioned like unto Christ's glorious
body,"—when the coming of Jesus shall
be the meeting-point and fulfilment of
His people's hopes and desires,—when
he shall be "for ever with the Lord!"

> " What must it be to dwell above,
>   At God's right hand, where Jesus reigns,
> Since the sweet earnest of His love
>   So brightens all these dreary plains !
> No heart can think, no tongue explain,
> What joy it is with Christ to reign.

" Where sin no more obstructs our sight,
    Where sorrow pains our heart no more,
Where we shall view the Prince of Light,
    And all His works of grace explore !
What heights and depths of love divine
Will there through countless ages shine !

" And God has fix'd the happy day
    When the last tear shall dim our eyes,
And He will wipe those tears away,
    And fill us with divine surprise,
To hear His voice, and see His face,
And feel His infinite embrace !

" This is the joy we long to know ;
    For this with patience we would wait,
Till, call'd from earth and all below,
    We mount to our celestial seat,
To wave the palm, and wear the crown,
And, with the elders, cast them down."

SWAIN.

Ballantyne & Company, Printers, Edinburgh.

www.ingramcontent.com/pod-product-compliance
Lightning Source LLC
Chambersburg PA
CBHW030643030726
47497CB00006B/1924